JESSUP

Stephen Ainley

MUD MEN PUBLISHING

*This book is dedicated to
the men who went to war,
and the men who came home.*

ISBN 978-0-6451666-1-3

Credits:
Front Cover Photo Courtesy of Leandro De Carvalho
(www.pixabay.com)

Cover design Cadhla Logan

MUD MEN PUBLISHING

First, they came for the Jews
and I did not speak out
because I was not a Jew.

Then they came for the Communists
and I did not speak out
because I was not a Communist.

Then they came for the trade unionists
and I did not speak out
because I was not a trade unionist.

Then they came for me
and there was no one left
to speak out for me.

- Martin Niemöller

Foreword

I have written many humorous tales over the years, including the Dennis Bisskit series. I got the idea to write a much darker story after a conversation with someone about the end of World War 2, and how soldiers returning home from years of trauma, were expected to just go back to normal life. Post-traumatic stress disorder and counselling were things of the future. And this is how Jessup came to be written.

Stephen Ainley

CONTENTS

JESSUP

Jessup gradually opened his eyes, but the pain was so bad that he immediately closed them. At the back of his mind, a voice screamed,

"Don't close both eyes, you idiot. Close the left eye and look down the barrel with your right."

It was far too soon after waking up for those sorts of memories. But still, it seemed practical advice, so Jessup opened his right eye, kept his left firmly closed, and amazingly, the pain was only half as bad.

He glanced at the clock on the wall.

1:15; that doesn't really help. Is it early in the morning or early in the afternoon? The curtains were closed, but daylight was attempting to break in around the edges.

So, it's 1:15 in the afternoon, and today is...Tuesday... no.... Wednesday. I distinctly recall that annoyingly chirpy chap on the radio this morning saying,

"Can you believe it? It's Wednesday already, halfway through the week."

Jessup felt strangely proud that he'd managed to deduce what day of the week it was, all on his own.

An empty bottle of Gordon's gin lay on its side on the table, and he tried to recall just what had led to this mid-morning party for one.

"It does you no good to open a bottle of spirits before sunset," his father had once told him. It was one of the few times he had ever spoken, but the more Jessup considered this advice, the more he thought there could be something in it.

He tried to stand, and the familiar pain shot up his leg, so he quickly sat back down. Strangely, there are some pains that even Gordon's Gin can't numb. A well-worn calendar was lying next to the empty bottle, which, on closer examination, told him it was June 14th, 1950.

"There you go then," he mumbled, "that's all we needed to know."

He heard a quiet cough coming from the corner of the room and suddenly realised that Marlow had been observing him during his painful awakening.

"Been drinking again, have we?"

He spoke in his normal condescending tone. Jessup suspected that Marlow already knew the answer, so he didn't bother replying. Then, after some time had elapsed, he struggled to his feet, gritting his teeth so as not to let Marlow derive any pleasure from his pain. Jessup took a deep breath, then grabbed his jacket from the back of the chair and said,

"Well, I'm afraid you will have to entertain yourself, old chap. I have work to do. Someone has to pay the bills."

*****

CHAPTER 1

As Jessup closed the door to his flat, he noticed Mrs Moss from the room opposite peering out of her doorway. He smiled, blew her a kiss, and shouted,

"You're looking especially gorgeous today, Mrs M. Anything exciting planned for the day?"

She shook her head and quickly ran back inside, slamming the door behind her.

As Jessup limped along Mile End Road, a young boy noticed him and tugged on his mother's skirt until she turned, spotted Jessup's face, and dragged the boy through her front door. He realised that he'd forgotten to wear his trilby, which he usually had tugged down low on his forehead.

Sod 'em, he thought to himself, *they are only scars.*

He continued down Westport Street and heard shouting as he neared the bomb site. A crowd of young lads were scavenging amongst the rubble for hidden treasure. It reminded him of when he had been released from the hospital in 1947 and gotten a lift from a porter to Cripplegate. The man had explained to him that there were few houses left, but Jessup had told him there was only the one he needed to see.

He had stood in front of his old home for some time, then an elderly man walking a tired-looking dog had appeared from nowhere and said,

"I don't believe it. Is that young Jimmy Jessup?"

Then the man removed his hat and added,

"Not seen you around since your mother's funeral, Jimmy. Here to see your father, I suppose, give him my regards."

He shook his head sadly before continuing, "That was a terrible night. The bombs nearly destroyed Cripplegate."

Jessup just stared back at him, trying to put a name to the face, and eventually said,

"I need to be alone."

The man nodded as if he understood and went on his way.

There was no sign that the bombed house next door had ever existed, just an empty plot of land. His father's kitchen had also been repaired, so he took a couple of deep breathes, crossed the street, and opened the front door.

"Just me, Dad, Jimmy,"

The house had been as quiet as a funeral home and smelt of decay. He'd stepped into the kitchen and poured himself a cup of water. Then, from his pocket, he had removed the bottle of tablets the doctor had given him, swallowed a couple, and tried again,

"It's just me, Dad, Jimmy."

His father was seated in his old rocking chair with his eyes firmly closed. Jessup looked at him for some time, attempting to discern if his chest was moving. The Germans had destroyed most of Cripplegate but had obviously been under orders to spare the old man and his equally ancient furniture. Suddenly, Mr Jessup opened his eyes and shot up from his armchair, shouting,

"Who's that?"

"It's me, Dad, Jimmy."

His father stared at him for a moment and then said,

"They want me to move out. They want to knock the house down and build flats. I'm not moving. The Jerries couldn't move me, why should I leave now?" Then he suddenly seemed to realise who it was and added, "What do you want? You can't move back in; there's no room. I keep my newspapers in your old room."

Jessup had felt dizzy.

"Why would I want to move back here? I nearly died, and you couldn't even be bothered to visit me in hospital. They have helped me find a flat; I just came back to grab my old clothes."

But his father had closed his eyes and appeared to have gone back to sleep.

Jessup walked through the house to the rear garden. The old Anderson shelter was still there, half-covered in soil and sandbags. Part of the opening had collapsed, and weeds had grown over it. He had the thought that if it were left, eventually, the shelter would disappear into the earth, and in a thousand years, archaeologists might find it and think what a primitive people we were.

The door to the garden shed had creaked loudly as he opened it as if no one had been in the shed for some time. Jessup spotted a rusty shovel in the corner. He levered up a concrete slab until he could lift it and scraped away at the soil beneath until he heard a clanging sound. The metal box was just as he'd left it.

After the battle of France and the evacuation from Dunkirk, Jessup had returned home on leave. His mother could not help but notice the change in him and had hugged him for a long time. His father had not even stood up to greet his son, just commenting that it was a sad day for Great Britain when hard-working fishermen and boat owners were forced to sail across the channel to rescue the military.

"An absolute disaster" had been his final words.

Before he had returned to rejoin his unit, they had failed to notice him enter the garden shed, pull up a slab, dig a hole beneath it and bury a metal container.

After a couple of deep breaths, Jessup carefully lifted the lid and stared at the pistol. He fell backwards, out of the shed door, and furiously punched his injured leg.

Don't think about it, don't think about it.

But it was too late.

***

He remembered the bullets flying over his head, leaping into the water-filled trench, and seeing the rats and the flies and the maggots. Then noticing the smell and screaming as he had realised he was lying on top of rotting flesh.

Jessup had scrambled to his knees and immediately vomited; God knows what, because it had been a while since he'd eaten.

The body was wearing a German uniform. Most of the exposed flesh had been torn away by rats, and hundreds of maggots were feasting on what remained.

Jessup looked away from the horrific sight but then slowly turned back because he felt sure that this was how he himself would die. Alone and abandoned in a muddy ditch, far away from home. Suddenly this pile of rotting flesh and bones was not the enemy but someone's son. Jessup had cried for the first time in many years.

Then he had spotted the Luger the man was holding in his right hand. Even in death, the soldier refused to give up his weapon until Jessup had snapped a bony finger to pry it loose.

When they returned to England, he had been given a few days leave. Jessup had wrapped the Luger in some dirty linen and shoved it into his pack. While he was at home, he placed the pistol in an old metal box and had hidden it in his father's garden shed because if his parents had seen it, they would want to know how it came into Jessup's possession, and that was a story he could share with no one.

Most of the lads took souvenirs home, some even live grenades. He had no idea why you would need something to remind you. The last thing Jessup needed now were memories. He punched his leg, shrapnel met nerves, and a sharp pain ran all the way down to his foot. It was an excellent way to clear the mind. The main thing was never to think.

Nothing good ever came from thinking.

Jessup had picked up the metal box and replaced the concrete slab. Then he walked back into the house and grabbed a couple of old shirts. His father was still sleeping, and after one final look around his old home, he had tucked the metal box containing the Luger under his arm, walked out and never returned.

***

He dragged his throbbing leg down Commercial Road, turned right and stood in front of the grim-looking building, with the sign outside announcing Arbour Square Police Station. Jessup took a deep breath, raised both of his hands above his head, and as he pushed the front door open, shouted,

"Don't shoot; I am unarmed."

The Sergeant who stood behind the reception desk continued scribbling down notes for a couple of minutes. Then, without even glancing up, he said,

"You're late again, and you look like shit, and I can smell the booze from here."

Jessup looked suitably offended,

"No need to be like that, Sarge. Something important came up, but I'm here now, and before you know it, those toilets will be so clean you could eat your dinner out of them. Although some of the food getting served around here, the toilet is the best place for it. It's amazing; I thought we won the war, yet we still have rationing five years later. I was reading that rationing is ending in Germany; what do you think of that?"

Sergeant Jack Prichard ignored the question for several minutes before suddenly looking up from his work and shouting,

"Don't start; I'm not in the mood. And talking of food, you can clean that vomit up in cell three. We had an overnight guest, and apparently, the porridge disagreed with him."

Jessup nodded,

"Not surprising, it's nearly as bad as that porridge we used to get in North Africa. God only knows what they used to put in that."

He turned and limped down the corridor towards the cells, and the young police constable who had been writing out a report in the corner of the room said,

"I don't know how that weirdo ever got a job here. How come you let him talk to you like that, Sergeant Prichard. He should show more respect; he's only a cleaner."

After not receiving a reply, he eventually added,

"And why is he always complaining about the war? He should be proud."

Prichard stared at the young man before replying.

"Oh, I'm sure he is, just as long as he doesn't think about it too much," then he asked,

"How old are you, lad? You missed out, didn't you?"

P.C. Barrett's face turned bright red before he blurted out,

"I wanted to go; they said I was too young. I would have loved to fight for my country."

Sergeant Prichard gave a wry smile,

"Well, that would have been a first. Funny how those that never went would have loved it. I've never met any that actually served say they loved it."

Then his tone softened,

"Listen, son. You were too young and I was too old, and we were the lucky ones. I served in the Great War and never wanted to see it happen again. I cried when my son marched off, and I cried when I got the news that his plane had been shot down.

"I don't know what Jessup's problem is and I don't ask. He's seen things that no man should see, and no doubt he's done things that no man should have to live with, so men like Jessup, I cut them a bit of slack. Now, young lads like you, I don't cut any slack, so get that report finished and get back out on the beat."

***

Marlow was in a foul mood when Jessup returned to the flat. Not wanting to get into an argument, he ate some cheese and mouldy bread that he found in the cupboard, then sat in the corner reading an old magazine.

Eventually, Jessup could stand the silence no more. He threw the magazine across the room and shouted,

"What more do you want from me? How many more times can I tell you how sorry I am?"

Marlow smiled at his outburst before answering.

"You made a promise, Jimmy. You promised to look after me."

*****

The East End of London, 1935

Jessup leaned against the lamppost, waiting for the exact moment. He watched as the old man polished the apples and carefully placed them in the wooden crate outside his shop. The man stepped back on the pavement to admire his handiwork, smiled, and turned to walk back inside. Just at that second, as his back was turned, Jessup quickly grabbed two apples and continued past the shop. Once he was around the corner, he placed one in each pocket of his jacket and whistled to himself as he strolled down Wood Street, towards the old Roman Wall.

As Jessup approached an alleyway to his left, he suddenly heard shouting and the sounds of a scuffle. Two men wearing dark clothing were attacking a young lad. He immediately ran towards them as the youth fell to the ground. One of the men was just about to kick his victim when he was grabbed from behind and thrown against the wall. Jessup had been taught to fight by his uncle, who could still be found standing outside some of the East End's toughest pubs, and seconds later, the two thugs ran off and disappeared between the buildings.

Jessup helped the unfortunate lad to his feet and watched as he wiped the blood from his face with his shirt sleeve.

"You'll live," he told him, "a bit of blood never hurt anyone."

The lad didn't seem inclined to agree but sat down and leaned back against the wall, breathing heavily for some time before muttering,

"I don't know why they picked on me; I was just taking a shortcut home."

"Blackshirts," Jessup said and then, seeing the confused look on the lad's face, added,

"You know, fascists, Oswald Mosley's lot."

He still had the look of confusion on his face, so Jessup asked him if he lived around here, and the lad explained that his father had died the previous year and he had recently moved to the area with his mother.

Jessup chuckled,

"You're joking, most people spend their life trying to get out of Cripplegate. I've never heard of anyone actually moving here."

The boy wiped his face once more and studied the blood on his sleeve before asking,

"Why would they pick on me, these Blackshirts. I don't even know them."

Jessup shrugged his shoulders,

"Are you a Jew? They definitely don't like Jews."

The lad shook his head,

"I don't think I'm anything anymore. My mom said if there were a God, we wouldn't be living here."

Jessup laughed,

"She certainly got that right. Oh well, it could be any reason. They don't like anybody really; I think they just like beating people up."

He reached into his jacket pocket, pulled out an apple and threw it to the surprised boy. Then he retrieved the other and took a large bite from it.

The boy munched hungrily for several minutes before suddenly wiping a hand on his trousers and holding it out towards his saviour.

"Sorry, I forgot to thank you for saving me. My name's Marlow, Harold Marlow."

Jessup stared at the hand for a second as if he were unsure what to do with it, then reached out with his own.

"Jimmy Jessup. J.J. to my friends."

They ate their apples in silence for some time before Marlow asked where they came from.

"Well, you wouldn't believe my luck," Jessup told him, "I was just passing Hobsons the greengrocers when I spotted a box of apples sitting outside the shop, and I thought to myself, Jimmy, I'm sure whoever owns those apples would want you to take a couple, and so I did."

They both laughed for some time before Marlow slowly dragged himself to his feet and said he'd better be getting home. He hesitated, then said,

"I hope those Blackshirts have gone."

Jessup stood up as well.

"Don't worry, I'm heading that way myself." Then he clapped Marlow on his shoulder and added, "Just stick with me, Harry, and you'll be safe as houses."

The young lad turned and smiled,

"Is that a promise, Jimmy?"

"Absolutely," Jessup replied, then spat in his hand and extended it once more. "And never let it be said that Jimmy Jessup broke a promise."

*****

CHAPTER 2

He slowly pushed the pile of dirt around the front office and tried to give the impression of a man fascinated by his work. But Jessup was far away, daydreaming about a time long ago when he had visited Brighton with Sally Foster and they sat on the beach and ate chips covered in salt and vinegar. She had gotten embarrassed and told him off when he suddenly kissed her.

When Jessup left for France in 1940, Sally had promised to wait for him, but a month later, she had written to tell him she met someone else and that they were getting married. It had been a pleasant enough letter, but now whenever he tasted salt, he couldn't help but think of Sally Foster's lips.

"Sometime today would be useful, Jessup." Sergeant Prichard suddenly interrupted his daydreams.

"Nearly done, Sarge," he shouted. "You will be able to eat your lunch off this floor, just got to sweep the corridor."

He limped around the corner, dragging his brush behind him, and too late, spotted Detective Sergeant Grimshaw and his young D.C. striding towards him.

"Oh, here he is, Hopalong Cassidy. Stop whatever vital work you are doing, hop along to the staff room and make me a mug of tea. You can make D.C. Thomas one while you're at it."

He saw Jessup hesitate, so he added, "Come on, Hopalong, unlike you, we have not got all day."

Then, as he limped towards the room at the end of the corridor, he heard the men laughing and then Grimshaw singing, "Run rabbit, run rabbit, run, run, run…"

Jessup filled the old saucepan with water, placed it on top of the stove and lit the gas beneath it. Then added three heaped spoons of tea into the pot. He noticed there was powdered milk but no sugar as it was still almost impossible to get.

While waiting for the water to boil, Jessup walked across the small room and tried each locker door. He caught his breath on finding one unlocked. After checking that the corridor was clear, he opened the door and looked inside. Some clothes were on a hanger and stank of cigarette smoke. Jessup suddenly noticed the faded photograph stuck to the locker door. It was Grimshaw and standing behind him, a skinny woman with a look in her eyes that he had seen many times: the look of fear.

He recalled the Sarge talking to someone on the phone months earlier. Evidently, Grimshaw's wife had turned up at the hospital with a broken nose, complaining that her husband had punched her. The next day, she changed her story and explained that she had made a mistake and actually had walked into a door.

On a shelf, there was a newspaper and beneath that, a wallet. Jessup limped across the room and once more checked that there was no one about, then returned and gasped on opening the wallet and seeing the banknotes inside. Reluctantly leaving the larger notes, he quickly removed ten shillings, replaced the newspaper, and closed the locker door.

Minutes later, Jessup flinched as Grimshaw spat a mouthful of tea onto the floor and shouted,

"Tastes like shit! That's not a critique of your tea making abilities, Hopalong. I'm sure it would taste wonderful if this rationing would finally end and we could get hold of some sugar. Now hop along; I'm sure you have a toilet to clean."

***

At two o'clock, Sergeant Prichard suddenly heard shouting coming from the corridor followed by a piercing scream. When he investigated, Grimshaw was standing over Jessup, with the heel of his shoe grinding down on the man's thigh.

"Pack it in, now," he ordered. "Jessup works for me, not you."

Grimshaw didn't move for some time and then delivered one more kick before backing away.

"He's a thief. There's money missing from my wallet, and he's always hanging around the staff room."

Jessup had curled up into a ball and was sobbing loudly. He slowly dragged himself to his feet, limped towards the Sergeant and gasped,

"I don't know what he's talking about, Sarge. You can search me if you want."

The Sergeant shook his head and said,

"Just grab your jacket if you have finished work."

Grimshaw turned and walked back into his office, slamming the door behind him.

Sergeant Prichard followed Jessup out of the station and asked,

"Did you steal his money?"

Jessup managed to look offended and answered,

"Of course not, Sarge. He's always picking on me for some reason."

Prichard stared at him for a while before saying,

"Listen here, Jessup. I know you had a rough time, that is why I gave you the job. But if I find you've let me down, I will have to let you go, do you understand?"

Jessup nodded, and the Sergeant continued,

"Grimshaw is a coward and a bully, and that's a bad combination. Between you and me, I also reckon he's bent. I can smell a bent copper a mile away; I just wish I could prove it. You better make sure you keep out of his way from now on."

***

Marlow was still in a funny mood, so Jessup made a big show of gently removing his right boot and then his sock. Reaching inside the sock, he pulled out a ten-shilling note, like a magician pulling a rabbit from his top hat.

"We are in the money, Harry. Let's go to Hattons, you know, that fancy restaurant on Oxford Street."

Marlow shook his head,

"I told you I don't want to leave the flat. I am not ready yet. You go; I'm okay here."

Jessup sighed,

"But you haven't left the flat since you came home; you have to go out sometime."

Marlow turned away. Apparently, the conversation was over.

*****

CHAPTER 3

D.C. Terry Thomas climbed into the passenger seat and wondered what his boss had in store for the evening. He had hoped to have a quiet night in with his new wife; she was already complaining about his long hours. The sooner she got pregnant, the better. Still, when Detective Sergeant Grimshaw tells you that you'll be working late, you don't argue with him. Truth be told, the D.S scared him.

"A little pub crawl tonight, son. Thursday is collection night, so it is time you got introduced to a few of the colourful characters around the manor."

Thomas groaned inwardly. Unlike most detectives he had met in his brief career, he was not a big drinker. He hoped it would not be a long night, but he smiled and said,

"Sounds great, Gov." Then he added, "Collection night? What is that?"

Grimshaw turned and stared at him for so long that Thomas started to sweat.

Eventually, the D.S. started the car engine and pulled away from the kerb, and with his eyes fixed on the road, replied,

"Never a good idea to ask questions, Thomas. Not if you want to live to be an old man."

By 9 p.m., Thomas understood what "collection night" meant; they had visited several East End establishments where they were handed bags of what he assumed was money. Prior to their first stop at The Ten Bells public house, Grimshaw had pulled over in a dark spot and told Thomas to join him at the back of the car. Once there, the Detective Sergeant opened the boot, removed two revolvers, and gave one to his junior, who just stared at it.

"I take it you have used an Enfield No.2 before?"

Thomas nodded,

"On the police firing range, of course, but why do I need one now?"

Grimshaw slammed the boot shut and said,

"Stick it in your pants and try not to blow your balls off. We are going into some dangerous places to meet some dangerous men. Any sign of trouble and I want to see that gun in your hand. No more questions."

Thomas didn't like it but knew it was best to keep quiet.

As the D.S. had suggested, they entered some dangerous places and met some dangerous men who had happily handed over bags of money. Grimshaw seemed happy with the evening's work and actually smiled as he told Thomas they had one more visit to make. He drove down Commercial Road and suddenly seemed even more alert.

"Okay, son, we are going to pop into The Mackworth Arms. Home of the Yids. They own everything around here; we need eyes in the back of our heads." Then he added,

"A word of warning. If you see a man with a giant scar on his face, for God's sake, don't stare."

The bar was surprisingly quiet, with just a few men in deep conversation, seated at tables. Grimshaw nodded at a thickset man sitting beside the bar. The man gave a slight nod in return and then disappeared into a backroom. The D.S. pointed to a booth in the corner and said,

"Remember: stay alert. I don't trust the Yids."

A young man bought them two beers even though they had not ordered anything, and moments later, a tall, balding man strode towards them. Thomas noticed that he had several scars on his face, including one from a knife which ran alongside his left eye down to his mouth.

As if by magic, a long knife instantly appeared in the man's hand; he leaned across the table and held the point against Thomas' nose.

"What're you staring at, boy? Something wrong with my face?"

The young Detective Constable tried to speak, but his mouth had gone dry. Grimshaw appeared highly amused by the situation.

The man suddenly smiled, and the knife disappeared as quickly as it had arrived. He sat down and said,

"Never stare, young man, it's rude." Then he turned to Grimshaw.

"And how is my friend today?"

The Detective Sergeant gulped his beer before replying,

"Fine, Jack. We are in a bit of a hurry, though."

The man smiled again, but there was no warmth in the smile.

"Always in such a rush, my friend." He nodded to the man sitting by the bar and the man rushed forward, carrying a small canvas bag, which he handed to Grimshaw.

When they were once again sitting in the car, Grimshaw burst out laughing,

"You should have seen your face when he produced his knife. I told you not to stare. Lucky you were with me; he's sliced men to pieces for less."

He drove for a few minutes before continuing,

"That's George Daw, otherwise known as Jack Daw. He runs the Jewish gangs around here."

He felt Thomas' eyes upon him, so he pulled the car over to the side of the road and faced him.

"Don't worry, son, there's plenty of criminals to go around, and you will arrest your fair share. But with some, the big ones like Jack, it's a lot easier all around that we have an agreement. If they keep things amongst themselves and not attract too much attention, we are happy to leave them to it."

He reached into the glove compartment, pulled out an envelope and handed it to the young D.C.

"You're part of the team now, Thomas. You will get this once a week, more when you have proven yourself. Just think, you will be able to look after that pretty young wife of yours."

Thomas stared at the envelope, unable to move until eventually Grimshaw dropped it in his lap, and added,

"Be sensible, son. You are either on the team or not. Look at Prichard, all these years, and he's still stuck behind the front desk, struggling to live on a sergeant's pay, all because he thinks he's better than us."

An hour later, Thomas quietly opened his front door. His wife, Shirley, was fast asleep, so he walked into the kitchen and sat down in the dark. His hands trembled as he opened the envelope that Grimshaw had given him and as he counted out the money inside. *Five, shiny five-pound notes.*

He knew he should go and see the Chief Inspector first thing in the morning and tell him that Grimshaw and God knows who else were corrupt and taking money from gangsters, but he also realized there was no way that could ever happen.

Thomas would keep quiet and try not to think about it. He would take his money each week, and in a month or two, put a deposit down on the house that Shirley had always dreamt of.

He hid the notes in a safe place and climbed into bed next to his wife. But sleep evaded him because he knew he had crossed a line, and there could be no turning back.

***

Jessup managed to avoid Grimshaw for the next few weeks until one Thursday morning when he shuffled out of one of the cells carrying a mop and a metal bucket. He exited the cell door and failed to notice the detective standing outside. Grimshaw stuck his left foot out, and Jessup fell headlong to the floor, tipping water everywhere. Hearing the loud clanging of the bucket, Sergeant Prichard stuck his head around the corner to see what had happened.

Grimshaw shouted,

"I don't know why you employ this fool; he's so drunk he can't even stand up."

Moments later, Jessup appeared at the front desk,

"He lied, Sarge; he tripped me up; I haven't had a drink in a couple of days."

Prichard did not seem surprised,

"Don't worry; I can tell when you're drunk. I can smell you as soon as you walk in. Just watch your step."

Then, seeing the cleaner's gloomy look, he asked him if he was busy that evening. At first, Jessup thought the Sergeant was inviting him out for a drink, but it turned out that Prichard wanted him to take the bus up to Whitechapel and pay his rent, as he had to work late.

The Sergeant handed him a brown envelope containing a week's rent, plus some change. Enough for his bus fare and a couple of drinks.

"Just a couple, Jessup. I want you here on time tomorrow."

Jessup went to the address Prichard had given him and handed the envelope over to the man who opened the door.

The man carefully counted the contents and then slammed the door in his face without a word.

Jessup wondered what the time was. He did not feel like returning to the flat yet and getting in an argument with Marlow, so instead popped into the first pub he came to, ordered a beer, and sat down in the corner. Looking up, he noticed the front page of a newspaper on the wall. Someone had gone to the trouble of framing it. Jessup smiled as he noticed the headline and stood up for a closer view.

"Do you think that is funny, my friend?" The voice came from a nearby table.

Jessup turned and saw an elderly man staring at him. The man was wearing the small skullcap commonly worn by Jewish men he had met.

"No, not funny at all, sir. It just bought back memories, that is all. The Battle of Cable Street, 1936, my friend and I fought there that day."

"And whose side did you fight on?" the man asked suspiciously.

"We fought against the fascists, of course, and we sent them packing with their tails between their legs."

The old man nodded.

"Yes, we sent them packing that day, but they didn't stay hidden for long."

Then he pointed towards Jessup's face and said,

"The scars, are they from Cable Street?"

Jessup shook his head and hesitated before replying.

"No, they came later. As you say, the fascists did not stay hidden for long."

The man stood up unsteadily,

"Well, young man, I thank you for that day and the terrible days that came later, and now I will now buy you a drink."

Jessup thanked him and watched him walk to the bar and order two beers. As the man turned to walk back, Jessup heard the door to the bar open, and someone enter. He glanced up and was horrified to see it was Detective Sergeant Grimshaw, alongside his young partner.

The old man, returning with their drinks, spotted the two police officers enter and how his new acquaintance quickly turned away, leaning down so that his head almost touched the table. When he reached his table, he kept one eye on the two men and saw a thickset man emerge from the shadows and hand them a small bag. They immediately turned and left the room. As soon as the door closed, he handed Jessup his drink and then said,

"Those men, do you know them?"

Jessup shook his head, and the man smiled,

"Of course, you don't. Neither do I, but I have seen the older man before on several occasions, and every time he stays for a moment and gets given a small bag. Sometimes he counts how much money is inside that bag, and then he leaves. Strange, don't you think?"

Jessup nodded in agreement,

"Yes, as you say, it is strange."

The man took a long drink from his glass then wiped his mouth.

"I think it is much better if you do not know him, my friend, because I think he is a very bad person."

*****

The East End of London, 1936

Following World War 1 and the economic collapse of the 1920s, The British Union of Fascists (BUF) had gradually emerged. Led by Sir Oswald Mosley, a charismatic speaker greatly influenced by Italy's Mussolini, the BUF attracted plenty of support in the early 1930s. Oswald raised his own private, 15,000 strong army, known as the Blackshirts, because of their dark uniforms. But as more Nazi sympathisers joined the party, it had become more radical and anti-Semitic, leading to outbreaks of violence at its rallies and a decline in support.

In October 1936, a planned march by the BUF in the East End of London was given the go-ahead, despite a 100,000-name petition being sent to the Home Secretary begging him to ban the march from taking place.

***

Marlow shrugged his shoulders.

"Why should we care about this man Mosely? If he wants to march against the Jews, so what? There are plenty of them around here. I'm sure they can look after themselves. Maybe if there were not so many Jews, we would have a proper job instead of having to beg for work anywhere we can find it."

"That's not the fault of the Jews," Jessup snapped angrily, "That is the fault of the government; they are

not interested in the East End, they are only there for the upper classes. That is why they are happy to turn a blind eye to Mosley and his thugs. If everyone is blaming the Jews, or the Communists or the workers, it detracts attention from the real people at fault: the government. You, of all people, should understand what the Blackshirts are like, or do you forget that I saved you from them the first time we met?"

Marlow remained silent for a while before saying,

"I remember it well, Jimmy, and I recall you promising to keep me safe, and now you want me to face thousands of fascists."

In a gentler tone, Jessup argued,

"And what happens after the Jews, who do they go after next? What if they decide that they do not like young men named Harry? What happens then?"

Marlow laughed.

"I don't think that will happen, but if it does, I'm fairly certain that the Jews will not come and help me."

Jessup smiled.

"Well, you are probably correct. Some wouldn't. Some would say, 'What's it got to do with me?' but I prefer to think that most would say, 'This is wrong, and we must prevent it ever happening again.'"

He reached into his pocket, pulled out an apple and threw it to his friend, and they sat in silence for several minutes before Marlow suddenly looked up and said,

"You know, I think it's a lot more likely that the Blackshirts would say we don't like young men named Jimmy. Especially that one that keeps stealing apples."

They sat on the dock and ate in silence for some time before Marlow made his decision,

"So, it looks like it's the East End versus the Blackshirts then?"

Jessup threw the remains of his apple into the water.

"Well, some of the East End, and it won't be just the Blackshirts. The police will pretend to be impartial, but when push comes to shove, they will side with the thugs."

His friend looked concerned, so not for the first time; Jessup slapped him on the shoulder and said,

"Just stick by me, Harry, and you'll be safe as houses."

***

Jessup gasped for breath and tried to push the bodies away from him. But more and more people seemed to be getting shoved into the alleyway. Just as he felt his legs start to buckle, a pair of brawny arms grabbed him and hauled him upwards and onto the top of a brick wall.

Once Jessup regained his breath, he glanced at the person who had saved him and was amazed to see the largest man he had ever seen. The stranger had arms nearly as wide as Jessup's waist. He sat with his legs dangling over the wall, casually watching the rioting protesters below, as though it were an everyday occurrence. He smiled, then spoke in a thick Irish brogue.

"Ya should be careful, lad. Ya wouldn't want to be dying before ya got ya first kiss now, would ya?"

Jessup wiped his hand on his jacket, held it up to his saviour, and introduced himself.

"Jimmy, Jimmy Jessup," adding, "I think you have saved my life, sir."

The big man laughed at being called 'sir'.

"Enough of that, me name's Padraig, but that's far too tricky fer you Sassenachs, so just call me Paddy. Everybody else does."

Jessup nodded and then leaned out as far as he could without falling off and tried to see the road running past the alleyway where the crowd had pushed him down. He heard them chanting "down with the fascists" followed by screams, as several police officers on horseback rode past, knocking protesters to the ground.

"Didn't take long for the bastard bobbies to choose which side they are on. They may as well wear black shirts like Mosley's thugs."

He leaned out further, and the Irishman grabbed his collar.

"Steady lad, have ya lost someone?"

Jessup nodded anxiously.

"I was with my friend, but we got separated in the crowds. We met up at Aldgate; I've never seen so many people. The fascists were outnumbered, even with the bobbies on their side. I heard that Mosley had decided to move to Cable Street instead, so I headed there to help build roadblocks. I got pushed down here... I hope Harry's not got hurt... I'm supposed to be looking after him."

***

Marlow was stunned by the size of the crowd. Thousands of people were already gathering at Gardeners Corner and more emerging from side streets. Up above, women were leaning out of the tenement windows to shout support. At first, he could not make out what they were screaming, but then the people around him took up their chant "They Shall Not Pass!"

Months earlier, Jessup had taken Harry to a football match at the Boleyn Ground to watch West Ham United play Newcastle United. It was the first proper game he had ever seen. Unable to afford tickets, they had climbed over a large wall to get into the match.

Harry thought it was the most exciting thing he had ever seen: thousands upon thousands of supporters wedged tightly together, chanting, and cheering happily as West Ham won the game, 4-1. Marlow thought he would never see a crowd that large again but today surpassed it. People of all nationalities and religions seemed to have forgotten their differences for the day and joined in one common cause: the fight against the fascists.

The crowd had been packed so tightly across the street that mounted police had ridden at them to clear a path for Mosley and his army. Most of the fascists wore dark uniforms and held their right arms raised as they waited for the word to continue.

At first, it looked as if they would succeed, but then, as Jessup and Marlow watched on in amazement, more and more locals flooded in from side streets and back alleyways. A tram drove across the street, completely blocking it.

As they were swept along by the tide of protesters, trying to avoid the horses, Marlow suddenly noticed a young dark-haired girl trip and fall, smashing her head on the hard ground. He pushed his way towards her, and as a massive police horse appeared in front of them, Marlow managed to grab the girl's shoulders and drag her into a shop doorway. He covered her face as a middle-aged man in a suit smashed the shop window with a large rock and then began throwing pieces of glass onto the road in front of the horses.

***

Jessup pulled himself halfway up a lamppost and scanned the crowd but could see no sign of his friend. He hoped Marlow had not been injured as he had seen several people being carried away, some covered in blood. On the far side of the street, he could make out a policeman on horseback surrounded by protesters, the policeman smashing some over the head with his truncheon in a vain attempt to clear a path, but there was nowhere for the crowd to go. Suddenly the man was dragged from the horse and disappeared beneath a volley of kicks and punches as his terrified horse bolted into the crowd.

As Jessup lowered himself onto the road, he began to hear shouts above the screams for everyone to make their way to Cable Street. Unable to pass, Mosley had changed the march's route and ordered his men to divert to the narrow road.

Jessup had tried to follow but was swept along by the vast crowd, pushed down a side alleyway, and eventually rescued by an Irish docker who had been sitting on top of a wall.

Padraig dragged him to his feet and shouted,

"Follow me, lad, I know a shortcut."

The Irishman was surprisingly light on his feet, and Jessup had trouble keeping up, sprinting along the top of the wall, then climbing a drainpipe and finally dragging himself up onto the edge of a building. Padraig had already climbed the steep slate roof and was resting against the old, blackened chimney, by the time Jessup reached the top of the drainpipe.

Padraig laughed, then shouted, "Hurry now, we will miss all the fun," and disappeared. Jessup was scared to look down and slowly dragged his body up the sloping roof. He rested a moment at the chimney, his clothes soaked in sweat and suddenly became aware of a cacophony of noise issuing from beyond the houses to his right. Through a gap he saw a seething mass of people.

After descending another even more precarious drainpipe, Jessup found himself in a long, narrow alleyway, with a wooden gate at the end. Padraig stood casually next to it as if he had just been for a stroll in the garden. Shouts and screams were deafening as the Irishman pulled open the rusty gate and then they saw what lay beyond...

A solid mass of bodies was packed across the narrow gap between the tenement buildings. Jessup glanced to his left: near Christian Street, the road was blocked off by abandoned cars, sheets of metal, broken furniture, and anything else that could be found. Above the shouts, screams and singing, he could hear a fragmented voice coming from a megaphone, ordering people to move now or risk arrest. A volley of rocks and rotten fruit from the protesters gathered behind the barricade instantly met the unfortunate officer holding the megaphone.

He suddenly realised that Padraig had disappeared, so he pushed his way through the crowds to get a better view. Nearing the barricade, he saw police officers climbing over the top of the obstructions, swinging their batons wildly at anyone getting in their way. For a moment, the crowd retreated, but one man fell to the road and was set upon by several policemen.

Without thinking, Jessup ran and leapt onto the back of the nearest officer, dragging him to the ground. This seemed to inspire the crowd and they quickly regrouped and attacked with whatever weapons they could find. Climbing to his feet, Jessup felt something warm splash onto his leg... He looked up and saw women, leaning from their windows, emptying the contents of chamber pots over the police officers. Moments later, the police turned and fled back over the barricade.

Shortly afterward, word reached the crowd that the police had ordered the march to be abandoned. A massive cheer erupted from the protesters.

Jessup felt a tap on his shoulder, and when he turned, Harry was standing behind him with a huge smile on his face. Next to him stood a skinny girl with jet-black hair and a determined expression on her blood-stained face.

"This is Maud. Maud Goodman, Jimmy. What a great day this is. I've never been so proud to be an East Ender."

Jessup glanced about him at the carnage and the many injured protesters being carried to safety. Then thought about the bravery of those who defied the might of the police and Mosley's army of thugs.

He slapped his friend on the shoulder and said,

"So, you've not been here for five minutes, and already you are calling yourself an East Ender." Then he smiled at Marlow's future wife, held out his hand, and added,

"I'm most pleased to meet you, Maud. Any friend of Harry is a friend of mine."

*****

CHAPTER 4

Pitch black. And Jessup knew a thing or two about the blackness. He had stood shivering, bowed down in a trench, and staring across no-mans-land, searching for the tiniest pinprick of light. But seeing nothing... Even the stars were too scared to come out. So black that he could not see the rifle he held in his hands. Just staring and listening for someone to make a fatal mistake. Because when it is that black and that quiet, the flickering of a match would appear to be a floodlight, and a muffled cough could sound like a drumroll.

But tonight was so much darker than any he had spent inside of a trench.

Tonight, there was total blackness, excruciating pain, unholy screams, and the realisation that they were his screams, and then finally he was awake...shaking and drenched in sweat with a migraine that felt like someone pushing a needle into his brain.

From outside his room, he heard Marlow shout,

"Keep the noise down!"

He slowly dragged himself up until he sat on the edge of the bed. He remained there for several minutes, rubbing the side of his head with the palm of his hand. Somewhere beneath the skin were pieces of shrapnel. Sometimes he thought he could feel one just beneath the surface. It was the ones he could not feel that were the problem.

The surgeon had told him,

"If they move too much, well..." He had shaken his head and walked off, leaving it to Jessup's imagination just what would happen if they moved too much.

Jessup stood... felt unbearable pain in his leg and screamed as he fell to the floor.

As he lay puffing and panting on the threadbare rug, he noticed the metal box beneath the bed... He dragged it towards himself, opened the lid and removed the Luger. It felt so cool to the touch that he held it to his clammy forehead to find some relief.

Suddenly the bedroom door flew open, and Marlow snarled,

"Will you keep the..." then he spotted Jessup lying on the floor holding the pistol to his head and smirked.

"Oh, so you are going to take the easy way out. Well, don't let me stop you." Marlow turned and slammed the bedroom door behind him.

Jessup stared at the Luger in his hand for some time. He was not ready yet, but eventually, when the time was right, he would place the pistol inside his mouth and pull the trigger. It contained two rounds of ammunition just in case he missed the first time.

***

"Working late again, Jack?"

Sergeant Prichard glanced up and saw Superintendent Muller standing by the front door, and as usual, carrying his shiny leather briefcase. Not for the first time, Jack wondered what was in that briefcase. Probably his sandwiches, he thought. Muller certainly never appeared to do any actual work.

"Bob's running late, but I don't mind. Plenty of reports to write."

Muller turned to the Sergeant and replied,

"You should mind, Jack. You have your wife Flo waiting at home. It might be time to call it a day. Retirement comes to us all in the end."

He smiled and continued his way.

Just a bit of friendly advice, Jack thought. So why did it sound like a threat?

After Bob Watkins finally turned up to take over the night shift, Jack walked home. Occasionally, if the weather were nasty or he was running late, he would drive. But it was only a fifteen-minute walk home. He had been born in the East End and knew these streets like the back of his hand. He doubted he would ever leave the little old two-up, two-down terraced house that became his and Flo's when his mother passed away.

He carefully opened the front door and winced as he heard the loud squeak his wife had complained about several times. It was one of many jobs she had mentioned over the last few months. Simple, five-minute tasks, but he could not seem to find the energy to do them for some reason.

Jack removed his boots, and there on the kitchen table, he noticed the plate of food and next to it the short note:

"Suppers cold. Gone to bed."

He stared at the plate of corned beef and cabbage for a while, then scraped it onto a sheet of newspaper, screwed it up and threw it into the rubbish bin. Jack quietly washed the plate in soapy water, poured himself a beer and sat back at the table, studying the note.

"Suppers cold. Gone to bed."

Years ago, it would have finished with "kisses" and "love Flo". Then a "wake me as soon as you get home"…

But now, the note was as cold as his supper.

Everything had changed on the day the telegram arrived, telling them their son was missing, presumed dead. He was only presumed dead because the military was very thorough. Even though many witnesses had seen the plane hit by gunfire, smash into the ground, and disappear in a ball of flames. Even though there was absolutely nothing left to find, the military would only presume him dead.

Someone had to be blamed, so Flo blamed him. Evidently, he had not tried hard enough to stop their son from going. Even though they had no say in the matter, like everyone else, Derrick had to go.

She had begged,

"You're a policeman, do something."

Even if he could have done something, Derrick's mind was made up. It was all going to be a big adventure, and it would all be over in a few months. Jack had recalled saying something remarkably similar to his mother in 1914.

He suddenly thought of Jessup. If his son had survived the war, they would have been about the same age. What if Derrick had come back like Jessup, a drunk, a petty thief. Scarred and broken by what he had seen over there. Stared at and ridiculed, reduced to mopping up the mess made by other drunks. Would that have been so much better?

But he knew what Flo would say,

"I don't care what state he came back in, just as long as he came back."

Jack drained his beer, walked into the sitting room, and sat down in the old armchair that his mother used to collapse into most evenings, worn down by twelve-hour shifts in the factory. He surveyed the room, the tattered sofa with patches on the arms, the scratched dining table, the worn carpet. Jack prided himself that not once in twenty-five years as a policeman had he taken a bribe, and God knows there had been plenty of opportunities. The only trouble was, principles do not buy you decent furniture, or a new dress for your wife so she does not have to keep repairing the old one.

Jack willed his eyes to look across the room at the photograph of Derrick, taken in 1940, smiling and handsome in his brand-new pilot's uniform; it was the last time they had seen him. The war may have dragged on for another five years, but Derrick's war had barely lasted six months.

Flo had hugged him for so long that eventually he had to pull away. Of course, Jack had just shaken his son's hand and said, "all the best" because hugging was not the way he had been brought up. Many were the nights he sat in this armchair, feeling jealous of his wife because her last memory was a hug.

Tears formed in the corners of his eyes.

"I should have hugged you," he whispered across the room to the photograph, "I should have told you how proud of you I was."

Then he closed his eyes in a vain attempt to sleep.

Nothing good ever came from thinking.

*****

CHAPTER 5

Jessup leapt back behind the old wooden fence and then carefully peeped over the top. He had managed to avoid Grimshaw for a few weeks and did not particularly wish to bump into him now. The Detective Sergeant had stepped out of the Police Station and decided to smoke a cigarette in front of the building. Jessup was quite happy to wait until he had moved on; but could not help but notice the man looked even more furtive than usual, glancing up and down the street and then behind him, back towards the station entrance.

Grimshaw glanced at his watch and then strode quickly to the phone box on the street corner. Jessup limped to the station as fast as possible and pondered why the Detective Sergeant would walk outside to make a phone call when he had a perfectly good telephone in his office.

Apart from a young constable staffing the front desk and Sergeant Prichard talking on the phone, the foyer was deserted. A detective suddenly ran around the corner and shouted,

"Has anyone seen the D.S.? We are moving out in a couple of minutes."

Jessup was about to speak when the front doors flew open and Grimshaw strode into the room,

"Just grabbed a quick smoke before the action starts. Out of the way, Hopalong, real men's work taking place here. I'm sure some vomit needs your attention somewhere." Jessup did not need telling twice, but before he could make himself scarce, several determined-looking police officers and detectives exited the briefing room, and moments later, the station was deathly quiet.

Jessup carried on with his work. The D.S. had been right about one thing; there was vomit requiring his attention, all up the wall of one of the cells, it appeared that the porridge had worked its magic once again. He cleaned the staff toilets, and then while sweeping the foyer, heard Prichard talking on the phone. The Sergeant slammed the receiver down, obviously unhappy about something,

"Everything okay, Sarge?" Jessup asked.

The Sergeant turned quickly and shouted,

"Nothing that concerns you. Get that waste bin emptied and get off home."

Jessup had never seen him in such a bad mood, and the reason became apparent once Grimshaw and the others returned to the station moments later. The Detective Sergeant had a big smirk on his face,

"Well, congratulations, Jack. That was a complete waste of time and money. I should imagine the Commissioner will want an explanation; you know how fussy he is about that type of thing."

Prichard was not about to back down.

"I don't understand it. My informant has never been wrong before. He was positive they would hit the bank at exactly ten o'clock. The gang must have been tipped off."

The foyer fell silent, and Jessup, who was standing in an office doorway pretending to polish the doorknob, felt his heart pounding.

Grimshaw moved closer to the Desk Sergeant,

"What are you saying, Jack? Because, if you prefer to take the word of your snout over my men and me, maybe we should discuss it with the Super."

The two policemen stared at each other for a moment, then Sergeant Prichard turned, walked to his desk, and sat down.

"I didn't think so," Grimshaw shouted. "Maybe you should let me have a word with your snout. You're getting a bit old for this game, Jack."

Prichard ignored him, so the D.S. stormed off to his office, slamming the door behind him.

Jessup quietly placed the waste bin back in the corner of the room, grabbed his jacket and walked outside. He sat on the small wall at the bottom of the entrance steps, let the cold air cool the sweat on his forehead and thought about what the Sergeant had said.

Someone must have tipped off the gang. He now knew why Grimshaw had used the phone box. That is the way it worked. The gangs did not hand over bags of money without wanting something in return. There was always a price to pay.

He knew he should tell the Sergeant what he had seen, but Grimshaw scared him. He was just a cleaner…why should he get involved?

Suddenly the front door opened, and Prichard stepped outside. He was just lighting his pipe when he glanced down and saw Jessup staring at him.

"Something on your mind, son?"

Jessup hesitated and then shook his head.

"Just thinking, boss."

Prichard slowly descended the concrete steps.

"Thinking? You don't want to be doing that, lad." Then in a kinder voice, "What you need is to find yourself a good woman. It does a man no good to be living on his own."

"Oh yes," Jessup snarled, "because I have so much to offer a woman. A drunken, scar-faced cripple who cleans toilets for a living. I'm surprised there isn't a long queue wishing to apply, Sarge."

Before the Sergeant could reply, he continued,

"Anyway, between you and me, I'm not alone. My best friend, Harry Marlow, is staying with me for a while, just until…" he hesitated, "until he recovers."

Prichard sat down upon a step, stared at his pipe, and muttered,

"I don't know why I smoke this; I don't even enjoy it, think I will go back to cigarettes" and then, "Sorry, I just assumed you were on your own. You always strike me as a bit of a loner."

Jessup smiled,

"Well, it wasn't always like that. Harry and me have been best mates for years."

The Sergeant nodded.

"Well, if you can't find yourself a good woman, a good friend is the next best thing. Recovering, you say?"

Jessup hesitated once more,

"He went missing in North Africa in 1943. Missing presumed dead, they said. It gave me quite a shock when he turned up, I don't mind saying."

Prichard suddenly felt faint. Missing presumed dead, just like their son Derrick.

"Was he badly injured?"

Jessup nodded.

"They did what they could in Africa; then he got sent to the Royal Herbert in Woolwich. It wasn't just the physical injuries; he had to spend some time in the Mental Ward there as well. Messed him up good and proper, Sarge, but he's getting better now."

Prichard patted him on the shoulder.

"Well, you take good care of him. Best mates don't grow on trees."

Then he stood up and turned away.

Jessup needed to tell him.

"Sarge."

"Yes?"

Jessup just stared until the Sergeant said,

"Well?"

Jessup gulped, then muttered.

"Thank you for caring."

Prichard placed his pipe in his pocket and shouted,

"The only thing I care about is that you turn up on time in the morning, not stinking of booze."

But the Sergeant had a rare smile on his face.

*****

CHAPTER 6

Two days later, as Jessup was leaving the station at the end of his shift, Sergeant Prichard called him back and asked him if he could drive.

Surprised, Jessup told him that he had driven a great deal before and during the war.

"Just asking because you seem to walk everywhere," Prichard commented.

Jessup scratched his chin and said,

"Well, cars cost money. And to be honest, if I owned a car, there have probably been a few times when I would have sold it to buy alcohol." Seeing the look on Prichard's face, he quickly added, "Of course, I'm not like that anymore."

The Sergeant nodded, hesitating before continuing.

"I have a friend, well, an acquaintance, really. George, George Crimmins. He's got a contract to remove rubble from the bombsites. Pretty busy as you'd imagine."

Jessup nodded in agreement. Wondering what this was all about.

The Sergeant cleared his throat. Whatever he was trying to say seemed to be causing him some difficulties.

"Look, you're a young man; you have your life in front of you. You do not want to spend it cleaning toilets. Anyway, the point is, the man who works for George is leaving in a few weeks. Moving to Scotland."

Jessup nodded again as if it all made sense.

"Look, I could have a word with him if you wanted the job. It would mainly involve driving the rubble from the sites to the tip. Hard work, but full-time work. Good money and a bit more job satisfaction than cleaning toilets."

Jessup stared at him, unable to speak. Eventually, Prichard said,

"Well, it was just a thought. If you are not interested…"

Jessup smiled,

"Of course, I am interested, Sarge. A real job would be wonderful."

The Sergeant pointed at his leg,

"Can you still drive okay with that?"

"Of course," Jessup confidently replied. "I only need one foot for the brakes. When do I start?"

"It's another four weeks before he leaves, so I'm afraid you are still operating the mop for a while yet." He stared at the younger man for a while before adding,

"I will be relying on you not to let me down, Jessup. If you mess up or turn up for work drunk, it will make me look bad, do you understand?"

Jessup looked him straight in the eyes and said,

"I would never let you down, Sarge."

Then he made an excuse to leave before the Sergeant saw his tears of gratitude.

***

Marlow ignored the smug look on his friend's face for some time, but when he started whistling an old tune, it was too much,

"Come on then, out with it," he shouted. "It is so long since I've seen you in a good mood that I didn't recognise it for a while."

Jessup feigned surprise, then carefully folded the newspaper he was reading and replied,

"I have a new job, Harry. A proper, well-paid job. Sergeant Prichard found it for me; he's a good man, Harry. He treats me like a normal person, not a scar-faced cripple."

Marlow did not seem convinced.

"But you are not a normal person, Jimmy. You will let him down, just like you've let everyone else down."

Jessup shook his head.

"I know I have let people down in the past, but this is my last chance to make something of my life; I won't let the Sergeant down. Only..." he hesitated before continuing, "Only, I think he is in trouble, Harry. Prichard is a good policeman, but there are some bad cops there, I worry about leaving him there on his own."

He stopped talking and looked up at his friend before adding, "I need to help him, Harry. I think if I can help the Sergeant, I can begin feeling good about myself; then I can start my life all over."

Marlow was shocked.

"Feel good about yourself? Start your life all over? Are you talking about redemption, Jimmy? I don't think it works like that. I do not think a person can do what you have done in the past and then just help some stranger at work, and everything is forgiven. I am no expert, but I do not think it is quite as easy as that. And what am I supposed to do while you are living this beautiful new life? Who is going to look after me?"

Jessup was disappointed; he had hoped his friend would understand,

"You know I will always be there for you, Harry. But you should not even be here. You should be with Maud, and…" Jessup's mouth suddenly felt dry "You should be with your family."

Marlow's ferocity took him aback.

"I've told you; no one must know about me until I feel better. You owe me that, Jimmy. Anyway, Maud has a new life now, just like you. It seems like everyone is starting over except me, Jimmy."

Jessup spoke quietly to calm his friend.

"I think you are wrong, Harry. Maud waited so long for you to return." he saw that Marlow was about to speak, so quickly added, "But if that is what you want, so be it. You know you can stay here for as long as you need to."

Jessup felt himself being weighed down by the atmosphere in the flat, so before his friend could reply, he climbed painfully to his feet and said,

"Well, I could sit here and chat all night, but I have to go out and find Robbie Marshall."

Marlow thought for a moment before saying,

"Young Robbie Marshall?"

Jessup smiled, "Well, he's not so young anymore; he must be twenty years old now."

"And why would you need to see him?" Harry enquired.

"Because I need to know something, and if you need to know something around here, you ask Robbie. Because Robbie knows everything about anything."

***

As usual, Robbie was seated on the steps at the rear of the flats, and as usual, he was wearing neither shoes nor socks despite the cold temperature.

Robbie indicated that Jessup should sit next to him and said,

"Long time no see, Jimmy. What brings you to the back of the flats? I assume you didn't pop around just to say hello."

Jessup smiled,

"Well, I do normally use the front door, but occasionally I like to check how my old friend Robbie is coping out the back. Still not wearing boots, I see."

Robbie lit a cigarette, exhaled an impressive smoke ring, smiled back, and said,

"You can't be too careful, Jimmy, now what do you really want?"

Jessup rubbed his leg, the pain seeming even worse now that winter was on its way.

"I need a camera, Robbie, and I need a film, and then I will need you to develop a photograph from that film."

One of the things that Jessup had always admired about Robbie was that he never showed any surprise in anything you asked him. He merely blew a few more smoke rings.

"And why would you be needing a camera, Jimmy?"

Jessup shrugged his shoulders.

"Does it matter? Anyway, you do owe me, remember?"

Robbie was quiet for a moment.

"No, I don't suppose it does. The problem is, I don't have a camera anymore, Jimmy. I used to use my

Uncle Gerald's camera when he lived with us. He was the one who taught me how to develop the photographs. Unfortunately, Uncle Gerald has gone to a better place."

Jessup glanced upwards, but Robbie shook his head.

"No, he's not gone that far yet; he moved to Brighton. Took his camera with him, I'm afraid."

Jessup stared into the distance, thinking now he would have to come up with another idea, but then Robbie interrupted his thoughts.

"Now, I think the favour I owed you has been repaid many times, Jimmy. But, as it happens, I know where you can obtain a camera, my old friend. In fact, you can obtain two. One for you and one for me, and I will develop all the photographs you want."

Jessup sighed. He had known that Robbie would want something in return. There was always a price to pay.

*****

The East End of London, January 1939

He had hoped that his father would be having an afternoon nap so as to avoid the usual arguments. But when Jessup opened the door, there he was, sitting in the old rocking chair that did not rock anymore, reading the same paper he had been reading since the weekend.

Jessup ignored him, smiled at his mother, and said,

"Nothing today, mum. They said they might need a couple of blokes tomorrow, so I will get down there nice and early."

He had been trying to get a job down the docks for the last few months, and every morning would queue up alongside hundreds of other men desperate for work.

Seeing the look on his mother's face, Jessup reached into his canvas bag, removed a long, green scarf, and handed it to her.

"Got you a gift, Mum. I know you've been feeling the cold."

His mother felt the warm wool and then held it against her face,

"Look, George, look what Jimmy got me for the cold."

Without looking up from his newspaper, Jessup's father said,

"Found it, I suppose." Before Jimmy could reply, he continued, "It's amazing how many things he finds. Apples, a jacket, even found a string of sausages the other week. You're a fortunate boy, Jimmy, finding all this stuff. I just hope your luck doesn't run out."

To quickly change the subject, Jessup said,

"Looking bad in Germany, Dad. This Hitler chap sounds dangerous. A few of the lads down the dock were saying we might be off to war soon. At least that will solve the unemployment."

Mrs Jessup placed the scarf around her neck, and in a booming voice said,

"Don't talk like that, Jimmy. We don't need a war. The jobs will come back. Anyway, Mr Chamberlain says it is all sorted out. He signed a peace agreement with the German chap."

Jessup shook his head.

"This man down the dock says it's not worth the paper it is written on; he says war is coming."

"And what will be the point in that," his father shouted. "I fought in the last war. The war to end all wars, evidently. And yet here we are, twenty years later, and people want to have another go. What good did the last one do? Certainly, it didn't help us East Enders, we were living in poverty before we went, and we are still living in poverty."

Mr Jessup suddenly stopped talking, raised his head and stared at his son. Jimmy felt that it was the first *time his father had ever looked him in the eyes. He thought he detected fear and maybe regret.*

"If you've got any sense, son, you won't go. The first sign of trouble, you should run and hide out in the woods and not bother coming back until it is all over."

The old man closed his eyes, and Jessup knew that was the end of the argument. Years later, he had suddenly recalled the conversation and wished he had taken his father's advice.

He told his mother he was popping out to see Harry, and as he opened the door, she had said,

"Don't get up to any mischief, Jimmy. I couldn't bear it if something happened to you."

Jessup strolled through Cripplegate. Men, surrounded by clouds of cigarette smoke, chatted on street corners while grim-looking women scrubbed their front doorsteps until they gleamed.

He heard a shout from above and saw Sally Foster helping her mother hang washing on the line that stretched across the street between the tenement buildings. Sally smiled and waved before her mother muttered something and she turned away. Jessup thought, if war was coming, he should hurry up and ask Sally out.

Jessup turned down a narrow alleyway between the buildings. He suddenly noticed a gate open and, out of curiosity, stuck his head around it. Just a patch of mud really, some scrap metal and a couple of worn car tires. His parent's back garden looked palatial in comparison.

An old shed stood in the corner, and without thinking, Jimmy opened the wooden door and glanced inside. Some coal in the corner. old glass jars, a broken shovel, and a canvas bag on the shelf in front of him. Jimmy opened it and saw the tools lying inside. A hammer, pliers, a saw. He suddenly realised whose shed he was in. Billy Marshall was a carpenter by trade, and while times were bad, he would often wander the streets carrying his bag of tools and knock on people's doors asking if they had any small jobs that needed doing.

For an instant, Jessup thought that he could make some cash by selling the bag of tools, but there was an unwritten rule. Cripplegate people did not steal off their own. So, he carefully closed the shed door behind him, and as he did so, heard a piercing scream that seemed to come from the front of the house. At that exact moment, Jessup smelt something burning and saw a plume of smoke escaping through the roof and flames appearing in one of the upstairs windows.

He tried the back door, but it would not open, so he ran as quickly as he could around to the front of the house. A crowd of people was gathering, and he noticed two women comforting Mrs Marshall.

Smoke could be seen pouring out of the old building's roof, then there was a sudden shattering of glass on the ground floor and flames forced back a man who had been peering through the window.

Mrs Marshall fell to her knees, screaming,

"My son, someone help my son!"

Robbie "Spider" Marshall... Jessup often saw him playing on the street in front of his home. More often than not, barefoot, even on a winter's day.

When he was five years old, Robbie had put a foot into a boot and trod on a big spider that had taken up residence there. Robbie's screams could be heard all around Cripplegate, and from that day on, he would only wear shoes on special occasions and only then after a satisfactory inspection.

A couple of men threw buckets of water over the front door and then tried to open it but were beaten back by the flames.

Jessup sprinted back around to the rear of the house, and without stopping to think, picked up a piece of metal scaffolding lying on the ground, smashed all the glass from a window and climbed through into the kitchen.

He immediately began coughing. Noticing a dirty old towel lying near the sink, he turned on a tap, soaked the cloth and held it over his face. The smoke was gathering near the ceiling, so keeping as low as possible, Jimmy walked across the room and opened a door he assumed led him into the sitting room.

Flames seemed to leap out towards him; Jessup jumped backwards. Then the flames appeared to retreat, so he carefully edged forwards, keeping so low he was almost on his hands and knees. The smoke was so thick that Jessup could barely see more than a few feet in front of himself. As he contemplated what to do next, he heard a plaintive cry from close by. All Jessup could do was feel his way around.

He tried shouting, but his throat was so dry he could barely part his lips. Just then, as Jessup was about to admit defeat, he once more heard a slight cry that appeared to come from right next to where he was struggling for breath.

Reaching out with his right hand, Jessup felt wood and then, as he ran his hand upwards, a doorknob. He turned the knob, pulled open the door a few inches and managed to gasp, "Spider..."

Nothing for several seconds and then a child's hand grasped his own. Jessup pulled the lad towards him, closed the door, and turned just in time to be drenched with water.

Just before Jessup collapsed, he saw the smoke part and a fireman emerge, as if by magic.

*** *

There had been talk of a medal for Jessup's bravery, but before long, people had far more important things to worry about. He spent several days in the hospital, and Spider, several weeks.

Afterwards, Jessup would sometimes get the young lad to run errands for him, and if Spider complained, he would say, "Well, it's the least you can do; I saved your life."

Within a year, Jessup was in France fighting German soldiers, but one day when he was home on leave, he spotted Spider sitting on some steps. He seemed to have doubled in size since the fire.

Jessup sat next to him, and after some small talk, Spider suddenly said,

"It was my fault, you know."

Jessup was confused until the young lad added,

"I started the fire; I was playing with some matches I found."

Jessup stared at him in amazement, but before he could say anything, Spider said,

"I saw you from the upstairs window. Creeping into our garden then into the shed."

Jessup must have looked shocked because the young lad suddenly burst out laughing.

"You should see your face, Jimmy. Don't worry about it. We all have our little secrets."

*****

CHAPTER 7

To save money, he'd walked all the way to Holborn, and now Jessup felt exhausted. He stood beneath a streetlamp to study Robbie's instructions. It was peaceful now; even Londoners needed to sleep sometime. Another hour or so and the city would burst once more into life, but by then, Jessup hoped to be tucked up in bed himself.

"Three a.m. That is always the best time," Robbie had said.

As if he would not know that. He had done enough thieving in his life to know that three a.m. was the best time. But he just nodded and said,

"Whatever you think is best, Spider," knowing that Robbie hated his nickname.

He walked past the Tudor buildings and the Royal Fusiliers War Memorial and almost missed the shop altogether, but luckily just happened to glance to his right...and there they were, in the middle of the shop window, two shiny new cameras.

Jessup bent down for a closer inspection of the square Bakerites, with Brownie Hawkeye printed on the front. Between the two words was Kodak, in tiny print, just as Spider had described them.

Jessup glanced up and down High Holborn and then stepped into the narrow alleyway next to the shop. The light from the streetlamps illuminated the first few feet, but then as he walked further, it was almost pitch black.

He removed the Army torch from his bag and shone it down the alleyway just to make sure no drunks were sleeping down there, then turned to his left, and just as Robbie had told him:

"Twenty feet down the alleyway, there is a window on your left. The curtains are kept closed for privacy but don't worry; no one will be in there."

Jessup hoped he was correct because he would hate to climb inside and land on someone's bed.

He quickly walked back and rechecked the street to make sure no one was around, then returned to the window, held his breath and smashed a pane of glass with his elbow. The noise sounded deafening in the silence of the night, but Jessup ignored it, reached through the broken glass, unhooked the latch and raised the window. He parted the curtains and shone his torch inside the shop, not surprised to find that Robbie was correct; the shop was deserted. After all, Robbie was always correct.

Jessup took his time entering, carefully placing the broken glass to one side before climbing through the window and stepping down into the shop. His leg had been throbbing and he cried out when his feet hit the ground and the pain shot through his body. He wanted to rest, but there would be time for that later, so instead, he quickly made his way down to the front of the building, relieved to see no one was walking past the shop window, then opened his bag and placed the two cameras inside.

He made his way back to the counter, stepped behind it and opened the second drawer down, and sure enough, there was a large box marked 620 FILM, just as Robbie told him there would be.

He stopped for a moment, wondering not for the first time, how Robbie "Spider" Marshall knew all this.

He counted out ten rolls of film, placed them in the bag alongside the cameras, slung the bag over his shoulder and with some difficulty, climbed outside.

One camera for him and one for Spider. He smiled at a job well done. Jessup had no idea how to operate the camera, but one thing was certain, Robbie would know. Robbie knew everything about anything.

***

True to his word, Robbie patiently explained Kodak Brownie Hawkeye's workings to Jessup, who immediately saw his plan's flaws.

He'd had the idea of catching Grimshaw in the act of receiving protection money. If he could somehow take a photo of the Detective Sergeant committing a crime, then he could pass it on to Sergeant Prichard, and he would have his proof of corruption.

Firstly, Spider had explained to him that before you took a photograph, you had to wind the film using a small wheel on the camera's side until Number One appeared on a screen at the rear of the camera. Before you could take another photo, you would have to repeat the procedure and wind until you reached Number Two, and so on. He very much doubted that Grimshaw would hang around while this happened, so it looked like he would only get one chance to get the photo.

Spider then told him that using the camera outside would result in a much clearer photograph, but an indoors photo was okay in decent light.

Seeing the look on Jessup's face, Spider placed the camera he was holding down on the table and said,

"Look here, Jimmy. I have no idea what you are up to, and I don't want to know; I have enough troubles of my own. But it seems that you would like to take a photograph of someone indoors without them noticing. Would I be correct? "

Jessup nodded.

"And does this person know you?"

Jessup nodded once more.

Robbie shook his head and then spoke gently as if he were having trouble explaining something simple to a child.

"You do realise that to get a decent picture, one where you can recognise somebody, you will need to be no further away than say, ten feet from this person?"

Jessup was shocked.

"I was hoping I could be much further away."

After a few moments of silence, Robbie said,

"I don't need to know, but if this is dangerous, then I would forget this idea."

***

On the following Thursday, Prichard asked Jimmy if he would mind paying his rent again as he was working a double shift. Once more, the Desk Sergeant gave Jimmy some beer money for his trouble.

Once more, Jessup went to the address on the envelope, handed the rent money over to the man who did not speak and wondered whether the man ever spoke to anyone or if it was just something about Jessup that he did not like.

He limped down Commercial Road, unsure of his intentions, then spotted the sign reading: The Mackworth Arms. Suddenly, concerned that Grimshaw could appear and find him lurking in the area, Jessup leapt into the doorway of a nearby tailor's shop and pretended to be studying a jacket in the window. He was contemplating what to do when a gentle voice behind him said,

"So, you are revisiting us, my friend."

He turned and saw the Jewish man who had bought him a drink on his last visit to The Mackworth Arms.

Not receiving an answer, the man added,

"Could it be that you are here because of the man you do not know? The man who collects money every Thursday evening."

Jessup stared into the stranger's eyes and saw a man he could trust.

Ten minutes later, he sat at a small table in a gloomy, one-roomed flat, while the man, who had said,

"Call me Bernie," boiled a kettle on a gas stove in the corner. He carried two steaming mugs across the room, placed them on the table and sat opposite Jessup. He apologised for the lack of milk and sugar, then said,

"Tell me what your problem is, Jimmy."

Jessup had no idea why he was here or why he would tell his secrets to a complete stranger. Still, for some unknown reason, he spent the next ten minutes explaining just who Grimshaw was and who Sergeant Prichard was, and then the plan he had devised to take a photograph of the Detective Sergeant as evidence.

Bernie sipped his tea and grimaced at the taste.

"This sounds extremely dangerous, Jimmy. Tell me, why would you risk your life for this Sergeant?"

Jessup pondered the question for some time. It was not quickly answered, so eventually, he answered it with a question of his own.

"Do you know what is so strange about the war?"

Bernie could think of many things, but he just muttered,

"Tell me."

"It only ended five years ago, but people barely mention it. It is as though, if they do not talk about it, it never happened, and the sooner it is forgotten about, the better. But the problem is, every day they get reminded of it by people like me. The scarred, the blind. Men in wheelchairs, men with missing limbs."

Jessup stared across the room for a while before continuing,

"Before the war, I would walk the streets of Cripplegate and men would stop me and say, "How are you, Jimmy?" Women would be hanging out their washing, and they would wave and smile. Now people just see a cripple with a scarred face. They avoid me because people will remember things they are trying to forget if they speak to me. And that is why I will risk my life to help the Sergeant because he treats me like a human being and not someone to be avoided."

Bernie just nodded, then stood up, crossed the room, and returned with a bottle and two glasses.

"I think we need something stronger, my friend." He filled both glasses and sat back down.

"Now, tell me about this camera. Remarkable things. I have seen one but have no idea how they work."

Jessup suddenly remembered and looked behind him for his work bag.

"I can do better than tell you, I can show you," he pulled out an old woollen shirt, unwrapped it and removed his shiny new camera, "I carry it with me in case I see something interesting." He didn't like to say that the real reason was he didn't want Marlow finding it and asking how it had been acquired.

For some time, Jessup showed the Jewish man the workings of the Kodak Brownie Hawkeye. Then from his jacket pocket produced several photos that Spider had developed the previous day.

"There is the old bomb site on Westport Street, and look, here is one of me."

Bernie was amazed.

"Remarkable. Who would have thought it was possible. The world is changing, my friend. I will soon be gone, but you must change with it; you must embrace it."

Then he walked to the small kitchen cabinet and returned moments later with several feet of brown twine. He passed one end through the camera's carrying handle, tied it to the other end, and placed the loop of twine around his neck. The camera hung down to his waist.

While Jessup looked on, wondering if the old man was perhaps losing his sanity, Bernie removed his long black coat from the hook on the back of the door, put it on, and buttoned it up. The coat was baggy and gave no indication that there was a camera beneath it.

The old man smiled.

"Perfect, yes, that is how I will conceal it, and then when the time is right, I will undo a couple of buttons, place the camera on the table, take a photo and hide the camera in my coat again."

Jessup leapt to his feet and shouted,

"No!" but before he could continue, Bernie held his hands up and asked Jessup to sit back down.

"Do you want to know why I drink in that establishment? It is because I always have drunk in that establishment. I was there before the criminals moved in, and I refuse to leave. I do not bother them, and they have no interest in me. I am just like a part of the furniture, no one notices me, and if they do, they just think it is only old Bernie dreaming of the past. And they are correct. I sit in there most nights and drink and wonder why I am still around."

He topped up their glasses and continued,

"In two weeks' time I shall be eighty years old. What a ridiculous age for a man to be; all my old friends are dead; my parents are dead. As far as I know, all of my uncles and aunts and cousins who lived in Poland have gone. Some on the battlefield and some in the camps, and yet here am I, feeling guilty for still being alive."

He removed a tattered handkerchief from his pocket and dabbed his forehead.

"I will take your photograph because you are a good man. And they will not notice me because they do not see me."

Jessup finished his drink, stood up and went to shake the man's hand but at the last second, instead placed his arms around Bernie's frail body and hugged him, just as he had hugged his mother the last time he had ever seen her.

Bernie showed him out, telling him to come to the flat early the following Thursday, and they would go over the plan one last time. Before he closed the door, Bernie called after Jimmy and said,

"When this is all over, we will drink again, and you will tell me how you came by your damaged leg and your scars."

Jessup nodded but wondered whether he would ever feel ready for that conversation.

He walked to the nearest bus shelter and sighed with relief as he sat down on the wooden bench. From his jacket pocket, he removed the container of painkillers and checked the contents: two remained. There was no way Doctor Jeffreys would believe that Jessup had accidentally spilled most of his tablets down the drain again. The doctor looked nearly as old as Bernie and probably should have retired years ago, but even he was not that gullible.

Jessup knew what he needed to do, and there was no point in putting it off any longer. The pain was unbearable and the tremors affecting his hands seemed to be worsening.

Before long, the bus arrived. Jessup sat far away from the other passengers and wiped the sweat from his face….

Thirty minutes later, he crept around to the back of the surgery and checked for any lights still shining upstairs. He guessed that it was around eleven p.m.

Much earlier than he would have liked, but he just wanted to get it over with.

As luck would have it, the back door was not even locked, and after carefully opening it just enough to squeeze into the house, Jessup stood and listened for a good five minutes. The moonlight entering through the windows was enough for him to see the staircase, and after limping to the bottom of the steps, Jessup stopped once more, and then, after reassuring himself that anyone in the house was fast asleep, he shuffled slowly towards the front of the home. Usually, when he had a doctor's appointment, Jessup would come in through the front door and enter the room on his right, so he moved slowly in that direction, spotted the sign proclaiming, "Doctor Jeffreys", opened the door and entered.

Taking a chance, Jessup turned on the light and quickly moved behind the large oak desk to the medicine cabinet. As he had feared, the cabinet was locked, so he searched through the drawers of the desk, but after a while gave up and sat down in the doctor's chair and looked around the office.

He thought about the times he had sat on the other side of the desk and faced the doctor and how forgetful the old man was. Once he'd been searching for his spectacles and Jessup had pointed out that they were sitting on top of his head. A man like that would not spend too much time hiding his keys for fear he would forget where he hid them.

Jessup suddenly stood up, walked to the kitchen cabinet, picked up the plant pot sitting on top, and unlocked its door with the key he found there.

He studied the rows of medications until arriving at the correct one, removed two glass containers with Morphine printed on their labels, and closed the cabinet door.

Then he had second thoughts, opened the door once again and removed two more containers.

*****

The East End of London, September 3, 1939

"Gas, gas, gas!"

She struggled to pull the straps of the mask over her head, took a few gasps of air, and then ripped it back off, crying out as strands of hair tangled in the rubber lining.

"It is no good. It stinks of rubber and I can't breathe."

Jimmy chuckled,

"You will be no good if we get gassed, Mum."

Mrs Jessup wiped the sweat from her red face.

"I don't care. I would rather be gassed than wear that thing."

"Oh no, you wouldn't," Jimmy's father's voice came from the corner of the room. "Believe me, you wouldn't, and it's not a joke, Jimmy. The government issued those masks, but I hope to God we never need them."

He turned away and Mrs Jessup winked at her son,

"You better get ready; Harry will be over soon for some last-minute support."

Mr Jessup raised his head once more,

"Yer friend chose a stupid day to get married on, here we are waiting to know if we are at war, and young

Harry Marlow chooses today of all days to get himself wed."

Before Jimmy could answer, Billy Hobson entered the room,

"Back door was open, okay if I listen to the news here?"

Billy lived by himself next door and, not possessing a radio, would often pop round to listen to the news.

"Of course, Billy," Mrs Jessup said. "Should be on soon; there's some tea brewing in the pot. Help yourself."

Before long, several other neighbours arrived; it seemed that people needed company today.

Moments later, the chimes went for eleven a.m., and silence fell over the room.

Everyone sat grim-faced in front of the radio as the news began. Suddenly there was a loud knocking on the front door.

Mrs Jessup half rose from her chair, clutched at her chest, and shouted,

"See who that is, Jimmy! Scared me half to death."

A few minutes later, Jimmy and Harry entered the room, laughing as they did so.

Mr Jessup raised a hand and shouted, "Shut up!"

They heard a solemn voice on the radio, instantly recognisable as the Prime Minister, Harold Chamberlain.

"...unless we heard from them by eleven o'clock that they were prepared at once to withdraw their troops from Poland, a state of war would exist between us. I have to tell you now that no such undertaking has been received and that consequently, this country is now at war with Germany."

The room was silent until Jessup said,

"Lucky you weren't planning on a honeymoon, Harry."

Seeing the glum look on his friend's face, he continued,

"It will be an adventure, Harry. Anyway, knowing our luck, it will be all over before we get sent anywhere."

Jessup suddenly noticed his mother was in tears and his father staring at her without moving. To Jessup he said,

"You're a fool, boy."

*****

CHAPTER 8

Bernie suddenly realised that the stocky man who always sat at the bar was staring at him,

"Feeling the cold, old man, why not move closer to the fire? Then you can remove that heavy coat."

Bernie ignored him for a couple of minutes before replying,

"I have sat in this chair, at this table; for twenty years; I'm not moving now."

The man at the bar shrugged his shoulders, mumbled, "Have it your way," and turned away. It was Thursday evening. He had more important things to worry about.

The Jewish man felt the sweat running down his body, and his hands shook so badly that his drink spilt onto the floor. It had all seemed so simple. Just point the camera and push the button, but now it slowly dawned on him that he could die in agony before the night was over.

*****

The East End of London, 1939

For a few hours, the shadow of war was forgotten, as Harold Percival Marlow married Maud Constance Goodman. Everyone in the neighbourhood attended the wedding and seemed determined to have a good time.

Harry's job as an apprentice tailor paid little money, and he had promised his new wife a wedding ring once he could afford it. But Maud was overjoyed when he had presented her with one he made from leather twine during his lunch breaks at work. She said that even if he gave her a gold ring covered in diamonds one day, she would always prefer this one.

It was a fine autumn day, so tables and chairs had been set up in the streets. Maud and Harry's mothers had spent the morning cooking, and friends and neighbours all brought what they could.

When speeches were made, Jessup had been unusually serious as he told of his happiness at seeing his best friend marry the love of his life. Then he told of how he had first met Harry. How he had come across him being attacked by Blackshirts and how Jessup had saved him. And then, to much laughter and applause, he added, "And I have been saving him ever since. "

Shortly after the speeches were finished, a loud siren sounded. Joey Green, who worked for the council, shouted,

"Don't panic! It's just a practice drill. I heard about it this morning," but some people left anyway, just to be on the safe side.

Jessup sat and drank warm beer with Harry while Maud danced with her father. Harry glanced at the sky and said,

"I hope Adolf doesn't try and ruin my day."

Jessup clapped him on the back,

"Don't worry, Harry; the Germans won't be here today. Some days you just get lucky, and this is one of them. Anyway, we will get to meet them soon enough."

Harry glanced nervously around and then said,

"Do we really need to go, Jimmy? As you said, it will probably be over soon anyway."

Jessup was shocked.

"What are you saying, Harry? Of course, we have to go. Do you want people saying we are cowards?"

Marlow shook his head sadly.

"I know, it's just that things are finally going well. It's my wedding day, and I have a good job. I want to save up, so me and Maud have a decent future…"

His friend just stared back at him, so he added,

"And what about you and Sally? You have regular work on the docks now. A few months, and it could be your wedding day."

Jessup burst out laughing.

"Me and Sally Foster? I don't think so. She told me yesterday that she would wait for me, but while I was talking to her, her mother ran out of the house and tried to hit me with her broom. I think I will be safer fighting Hitler."

Harry joined him in his laughter, but Jimmy knew he was still worried, so he said,

"A quick adventure, a few laughs, and we will be back as heroes before you know it. And one day, when there is a little Harry, you will be able to tell him that when you were called, you fought for your country. Just think how proud he will be."

Marlow smiled at last,

"You are right as usual, Jimmy. Won't that be a great day..."

Jessup nodded,

"Don't forget to tell him that, also, as usual, my best friend, Jimmy, had to get me through it."

*****

CHAPTER 9

Bernie could not divert his eyes from the clock on the wall. His hands shook so violently that when he had tried to pay the barman, the coins had fallen to the floor.

The stocky man sitting at the bar had turned, sneered, and said,

"Drunk already, old man. Maybe it's time you went home to your memories."

At seven-thirty, the doors to the bar flew open, and the man Jessup had named Detective Sergeant Grimshaw entered and strode confidently across the room to his usual table.

Bernie stared straight ahead, but beneath the table, fumbled at the buttons on his coat.

Grimshaw nodded at the stocky man sitting at the bar, and the man slowly rose from his stool, walked across the room, and disappeared up the staircase.

Bernie had managed to undo one button but struggled with the next one. His heart was beating so loudly that he felt sure Grimshaw must hear it.

He suddenly felt the bottom of his coat come loose. He quickly pinched it closed but could feel the camera with his fingertips.

The stocky man returned carrying a bag, and just behind him, the tall man with the ugly face and the long knife scar running down the side of it, looking as if he did not have a care in the world because this was the centre of his kingdom and no one would ever dare to cross him here.

Bernie gently rocked backwards and forwards, thinking that he might wet himself any second. His mind told him to just forget all about it, he did not owe this young man anything, but his hands betrayed him, lifted the camera to the table, and positioned it behind his hat.

He pretended to reach for his drink but instead rested his hand on top of the camera, and not daring to glance down, felt around for the button. Jessup had said the photograph was only good if the man with the scar was handing the bag to Grimshaw.

Bernie watched them carry on awkward small talk, and then the gangster picked up the bag and leaned across the table towards the Detective Sergeant. As the sweat dripped from his face, the old Jewish man felt for the button when suddenly, Grimshaw spun around and shouted,

"What are you staring at?"

Bernie just looked straight ahead as if he had not heard the question and felt warm liquid run down his legs.

Jack Daw spun around with his knife ready in his hand and then burst out laughing,

"It's just old Bernie. You don't see anything, do you, Bernie?"

The old man remained still as if he were asleep.

"See. Bernie is just part of the furniture."

The stocky man moved closer, and a look of disgust came over his face.

"I knew he was drunk; he's pissed himself. Come on, you old fool, get off home."

Jack Daw roared with laughter as Bernie looked up as if he had just awoken. He picked up his hat, pushed back his chair, and left without a word.

Once outside, Bernie pulled his coat closer, ashamed that someone might see the wet patches on his trousers. He shuffled along the pavement until he reached his flat, and only once the door was locked behind him did he remove the camera from inside his hat.

Still trembling, Bernie sat on the edge of his bed and shed tears, for the fear he felt when Grimshaw had shouted at him and tears of pride because, despite being afraid, he managed to push the button on the camera.

He bathed himself and changed into dry clothes and an hour later heard a tap on his door.

"It's just me: Jimmy."

Bernie looked even frailer than the last time Jessup had seen him, and he felt guilty for asking so much of the old man as he handed him the camera.

"I have done all I can do for you, my friend. I took your photograph, but I have no idea if it will help you, I'm afraid I had my eyes closed as I took it."

Jessup understood and nodded as he placed the camera in his bag, then hugged Bernie. As he turned to leave, Bernie grabbed his arm.

"You are still young, Jimmy. You should forget all this and live your life."

The younger man nodded once more and left. Bernie felt sad because he doubted that his advice would be heeded.

***

Spider stared at the camera,

"What do you mean you don't want it anymore?"

Jessup shrugged his shoulders,

"Why would I need a camera? All I need is this photograph developing; you can keep the camera."

Spider seemed suspicious as if fearing a trap,

"And who is in this photograph?"

Jessup shrugged his shoulders,

"Does it matter?"

Robbie "Spider" Marshall smiled,

"No, I don't suppose it does. But I'm a bit busy at the moment. Come back on Tuesday, and I should have something for you."

CHAPTER 10

Jimmy could feel the atmosphere inside the station. Sides had been taken. Many thought that Sergeant Prichard had overstepped the mark by insinuating that someone on the force would be tipping off criminals.

The Sergeant just got on with his job and ignored the whispers until mid-morning, when Superintendent Muller asked to see him.

The Super smiled as he poured Prichard a mug of tea.

"Just a friendly chat, Jack. Off the record, of course."

He handed the Desk Sergeant his tea and continued,

"I had Grimshaw in here, a bit upset; you know what he's like...says you were making accusations."

Jack just stared back at him, so the Super carried on,

"Look, Jack, we've known each other...well...it must be twenty years."

"Twenty-two years," Jack interrupted.

Superintendent Muller smiled.

"Twenty-two years? Well, there you go, that is a long time. Anyway, I don't want any bad blood in the station. It might be best if you apologise to him. Unless, of course, you have some kind of proof. I mean, if someone here was up to no good, you know you can rely on me to stamp on it immediately, Jack."

The Desk Sergeant placed his mug of tea on the table, stood up and said,

"I have no proof. But I won't be apologising to Grimshaw. He's a bad cop. I've been around long enough to know one when I see one."

As he turned to leave, the Superintendent said,

"Be careful, Jack. Grimshaw does a good job, but he is a vindictive man. You will be retiring soon; no point in making waves."

***

Jessup noticed that the Sarge seemed preoccupied, so he waited until afternoon to disturb him,

"Sarge."

"Yes?"

"I was just wondering..."

"Well, out with it."

"I was just wondering if I could borrow your car?"

Sergeant Prichard glanced up from his reports,

"Borrow my car?"

Jessup edged closer to the reception desk,

"Well, it's like this, Sarge. I know how to drive and everything, it's just…"

"Get to the point, Jessup. These reports won't write themselves."

"It's just that I haven't driven for a long time. I would like a little practice before I start my new job."

Prichard stared at him for a while and then glanced at the clock on the wall,

"I finish in thirty minutes. Wait for me in the car park. I'm not letting you loose with my car on your own, but you can take me for a drive."

Jessup was standing next to the Sergeant's gleaming Morris Eight when he appeared.

"Hope you haven't scratched it, Jessup," he shouted, "that's my pride and joy."

Jessup could not help but smile,

"I never even touched it, Sarge. I was worried that it might fall to pieces. Is it not time you invested in a newer model?"

The sergeant pretended to be annoyed,

"Less of your cheek, lad. The car will see me through for the rest of my days. Just remember any damage comes out of your pay."

Jessup climbed into the driver's seat. The sergeant lowered the sun visor and caught the keys as they fell. He passed them to Jessup, who started the engine.

"Anywhere special, boss?"

"Let's go down to Limehouse. Do you know The Grapes?"

Jessup nodded.

"I used to work on the docks. Everyone knows The Grapes."

"Used to be my local. Not been in there for years. I feel like watching the traffic on the river and drinking a pint. You can have a lemonade being as you are my chauffeur."

He gestured for Jessup to move and then grimaced as the car bounced across the car park several times, narrowly missing a couple of vehicles before swerving onto the main road.

Once they reached The Grapes, the Sergeant relented and said,

"One beer, and that's all. Your driving is bad enough when you are sober."

They grabbed their drinks and sat on the balcony overlooking the River Thames. The peace was only interrupted by bulldozers clearing rubble nearby.

Prichard took a gulp of beer, licked his lips, then said,

"The last time I was down this way was when the King and Queen visited after the bombing. I was on duty, and they came over and spoke to me. They were just down-to-earth as if they were East Enders. They could not believe the damage. Do you know what is amazing? They bombed all around St. Pauls, but they couldn't destroy it, and they bombed all around The

Grapes, and they couldn't destroy it either." He raised his glass and added, "The Lord moves in mysterious ways."

Jessup smiled, enjoying his day out. He watched the Sarge expertly roll a cigarette.

"I suppose you want one?"

Jessup hesitated, then shook his head,

"I used to smoke, but I stopped..." He suddenly reached across the table and picked up the cigarette, "I will just hold it if that's okay?"

Prichard stared at him for some time.

"I hope you won't be offended by me saying this, but you really are a strange man."

Jessup smiled.

"No offence taken, Sarge. I like to hold them but can't stand the taste anymore."

*****

France, 1940

Marlow was in a bad mood as usual,

"Some adventure this turned out to be. And I thought you said we would see France. All I've seen so far is the inside of a truck and the inside of a trench."

Jessup smiled at his friend,

"Well, no one at home will know that. You will be able to tell Maud you saw France, and if you stand up and look to the North, you will be able to tell her you saw Belgium as well."

Big Ron laughed out loudly at this but added,

"That's true, but I wouldn't advise you to stand up, or you might not make it back home to tell Maud all about your holiday abroad."

There was silence as the big man expertly rolled three thin cigarettes, passed them around, and said,

"Now, let's see if you thick east-enders can finally get the hang of it."

He drew in a mouthful of smoke and then opened his mouth in an 'o' shape, and a ring of smoke emerged, closely followed by several more. They floated along the trench, teasing Marlow, who had burst into a fit of coughing at the first attempt.

"Look at this one; it's a beauty," Jessup shouted proudly.

Big Ron nodded in admiration,

"Looks like the challenge is on."

He took a deep drag of tobacco, leaned back, and opened his mouth. The largest smoke ring they had ever seen drifted upwards, the sun making it appear like an angel's halo.

Big Ron stood up excitedly, pointing towards his miraculous achievement.

Jessup laughed as a small hole appeared in his comrade's forehead and only stopped when Ron slid to the floor of the trench and fell forwards, revealing the back of his head was missing.

They stared at the body of their dead friend for some time, and then Jessup spat out the blood-soaked cigarette from his mouth and vomited over Big Ron's boots.

*****

CHAPTER 11

"How's that friend of yours?" Prichard suddenly asked, "Marlow, wasn't it?"

Jessup sipped his pint slowly, hoping to impress the Sergeant.

"Yes, Sarge, Harry Marlow. He's...well... these things can take time."

Prichard nodded, not wanting to pry.

Jessup suddenly came to a decision,

"Sarge, there is something I need to tell you."

Sergeant Prichard had been watching a small boat navigate the river but turned his head sharply,

"I hope you haven't changed your mind; I told my friend you definitely wanted the job."

Jessup hesitated.

"It's not that, Sarge; I still want that job. It's just something I saw, and it might be important. I was outside the station trying to avoid Grimshaw that morning when the bank robbery was supposed to take place."

The sergeant set his beer glass on the table,

"And?"

"Well, it might be nothing, but Grimshaw was out the front looking around. You know, as if he were checking if anyone was watching. Then he went to the phone box on the corner and made a call."

Prichard just stared at him, so Jessup continued,

"The point is, Sarge, when he came in he said he had been having a smoke. He never mentioned anything about a phone call."

Sergeant Prichard rubbed his eyes for a moment and suddenly seemed older.

"I appreciate you telling me, lad. Now just forget all about it; it isn't your fight."

Jessup decided not to mention seeing Grimshaw in The Mackworth Arms or Bernie attempting to take a photograph. He knew the Sergeant would be angry with him for getting involved. To change the subject, he asked if the Sarge had always wanted to be a policeman.

Prichard thought for a moment.

"I can't recall ever wanting to do anything else. My dad was a policeman for over thirty years and would have carried on as well if he hadn't gotten sick. It was just expected that is what I would do. I never regretted it, well, not until the last year or so."

He hesitated as if unsure what to say in front of Jessup,

"There have always been cops that strayed outside the rules. There was nothing wrong with giving someone a clip around the ear when you arrested them. But you would always get someone who would go too far because they enjoyed it too much. Or the cop who would accept free drinks in exchange for turning a blind eye if closing time ran a bit late. But it has all changed now. When you cannot tell the difference between the police and the gangsters, it's not the police force I joined."

He sighed, wondering if he had said too much.

"Well, that's enough about me. What about you? Did you always aspire to be a toilet cleaner?"

*****

France 1940

Jessup stared into the cracked mirror and tried to recognise the stranger looking back at him. Eventually, he gave up and turned his attention to the bucket of muddy water beside him. A thin layer of ice had formed across the top of the liquid, so he smashed it with his fist, cupped his hands with the icy cold water then splashed it over his face and gasped,

"Can't we just light a small fire?"

Corporal Wilkins was sitting cross-legged on the concrete floor, cleaning his rifle. He removed a spring from his mouth and answered,

"No, we can't risk anyone seeing smoke. Anyway, George and Tommy should be back soon from scouting the road. If they say it is all clear, we will move out once it's dark."

Someone tapped Jessup on the shoulder; he turned, and Marlow handed him a muddy potato with green shoots sprouting from it.

"Found a bag in the cellar," he mumbled.

Marlow still looked like a choirboy. Far too young to be in this hellhole, surrounded by death. Not for the first time, Jessup felt a tinge of guilt. Everyone looked too young to be here, but especially Harry.

"I wouldn't recommend eating those," Wilkins shouted. 'They could make you ill."

Jessup bit his potato in half and chewed it slowly.

"I'm already ill. At least I will be ill with something in my stomach."

Seconds later, Jessup vomited his snack, rinsed his mouth in the muddy water, then stared through a window across the field in front of the dilapidated farmhouse.

In the centre of the field, several crows feasted on the remains of a dead cow. When they had arrived at the farm, Jessup suggested a couple of them crawl across the field to the cow and take some of the meat, but Corporal Wilkins said it was too dangerous to risk, as there could be a sniper up in the hills overlooking the property.

As they cleaned their weapons, Jessup had surprised them all by stating that he would like to be a farmer once the war was over.

Pete Mckue had laughed so hard he almost choked.

"What do you know about farming, Jimmy?"

Marlow had joined in the laughter.

"Well, he stole a couple of pork chops once. I was supposed to keep watch outside the butcher's shop, but a pretty girl walked past, and I watched her instead. Suddenly, Jimmy came running past me with pork chops in his hand and the butcher chasing him with a big knife in his. It's a good job Jimmy is a good runner, or else he wouldn't be with us today."

Even Corporal Wilkins was amused by the tale and commented,

"I could be wrong, Jimmy, but I don't think stealing a couple of pork chops makes you a farming expert."

For once, Jessup did not smile.

"Just a dream, lads. A pretty wife, a couple of kids, a dog, a farm with a few animals. Just a dream, I will probably end up cleaning toilets."

Suddenly their chat was interrupted by the sound of gunfire in the distance.

Corporal Wilkins screamed, "Stand to!" grabbed his Lee-Enfield and raced to the nearest window and smashed out a pane...

"I hope that's not our lads."

Jessup ran for the door, shouting,

"Come on! They could be in trouble!"

"Wait! Stay where you are, lads! It may have nothing to do with us."

Jessup reluctantly returned to his post and stared out across the field.

Minutes later, Corporal Wilkins shouted,

"It looks like George! He's dragging something... Jimmy, with me, the rest of you cover us."

They raced out of the building, their rifles ready, and sheltered behind a rusty tractor with the front wheels missing. After a moment, they saw George appear next to the dead cow. He spotted them and cried out,

"They killed Tommy! I couldn't carry him..."

...A single shot rang out, and George slowly crumbled onto the carcass.

When darkness fell, Wilkins asked for a volunteer, and as usual, Jessup was the first to raise his hand.

They crawled across the field until they reached the bodies. Before sunrise, they buried Tommy and George near an old shed, placed a wooden cross on their graves, and were gone by the time daylight arrived...heading towards the coast to a small seaside town called Dunkirk.

Jessup had decided he did not wish to be a farmer after all.

*****

CHAPTER 12

Bright red. Jessup couldn't believe it. When he sat down in the deckchair and closed his eyes, it had been a sunny, clear day, and now, seconds later, a bright red mist approached, moving closer and closer until he could barely see a short distance in front of himself. Moments later he was utterly enveloped by the mist...He opened his mouth, and screamed at the taste...

Jessup awoke, hanging half out of bed. He rose quickly, spat several times and then, spotting a half-empty mug of cold tea next to the bed, gulped down the contents and sat, panting loudly, until he heard a loud, "Shut up!!" from Marlow's room.

A half-hour later, he left his flat without even bothering to check on his friend. If Marlow could not learn to be civil, he could look after himself.

Five minutes later, he spotted Robbie Marshall striding towards him, barefoot as usual.

"Morning, Spider, you're up and about early today..."

But Robbie didn't answer, instead looked up and down the street, as if checking no one was watching, and then indicated Jessup should follow him down a nearby alleyway.

Robbie walked down the narrow gap between buildings and waited near several overfilled rubbish bins. When Jessup arrived, Robbie grabbed him by the lapels of his jacket, flung him against the wall and hissed,

"What's your game, Jimmy? What have you got me into?"

Jessup stared at him for a moment before answering.

"I don't know what you are talking about, Spider, but if you don't let go of my jacket, I am going to punch you so hard that you won't wake up until tomorrow."

Robbie reluctantly dropped his hands to his sides, took a couple of deep breaths, removed something from his pocket, and held it up so Jessup could see.

"I thought you were just taking a photo of a girl you liked. Something a bit artistic, not this. This can get us both killed, Jimmy."

Jessup stared at the photograph and could barely believe it. The man on the right was handing a bag to the man on the left and he had turned to face the camera. It was as if Bernie had shouted, "Say cheese," and Detective Sergeant Grimshaw had smiled for the camera. Except instead of smiling, he was scowling. Still, that didn't matter…the important thing was, there was no mistaking it was Grimshaw in the photo.

Jessup laughed loudly.

"That's brilliant, Spider."

Robbie shook his head, "No, it isn't brilliant, Jimmy. Do you know who that man is?"

Jessup smiled.

"Of course, I do. He's a detective at the station where I work."

"Not him," Robbie shouted and then glanced around to make sure no one could hear him.

"I couldn't care less who *that* is; I'm talking about the other man."

Jessup took another look at the photo. The man on the right had barely registered in his mind. Now he saw that the man handing Grimshaw the bag was also just starting to turn towards the camera. His left hand was just removing something from his jacket and when Jessup looked closer, he could make out a glint of metal.

"So, who is he, a friend of yours?"

Spider shook his head.

"I've never met him, and I would prefer to keep it like that. But I know who it is. That's George Daw, better known as Jack Daw. Do you get it? Jack Daw, like the bird."

"Of course, I get it, Robbie. I'm a cripple, not an idiot. What about him?"

Spider took a deep breath and seemed to calm down.

"I'm assuming he didn't see you take the photo, or else you wouldn't be alive today. Now, personally, I would prefer to live a long life, so I think the best thing to do is tear that photo up and burn it."

He reached out, but Jessup quickly tucked the photo inside his jacket pocket.

"You don't need to concern yourself, Robbie. There is nothing to connect you to this photograph. I didn't even take it, someone else did, and they were not seen. So, I think the best thing for you to do is to forget you ever saw it and go and play with your nice new cameras."

Robbie didn't move for a few minutes. When he finally walked away, he turned back after a few steps and said,

"Any debts I owed you are all paid, Jimmy. I just hope you know what you are doing."

**

Jessup waited until there was no one else in the reception room and then caught the attention of Sergeant Prichard,

"I need to show you something, Sarge. Could we meet somewhere quiet at lunch?"

The Desk Sergeant put down the reports he was working on and stood up,

"Look, Jessup. Just because we had a pint and a chat yesterday doesn't make us best friends. Nothing against you, but I like to eat my sandwiches in peace."

Jessup was adamant.

"It is really important, Sarge." He looked so desperate that the Sergeant relented and said,

"Just this once. Meet me by my car at midday."

Jessup was waiting when the Sarge turned up and invited him into the passenger seat.

Sergeant Prichard opened his glove compartment and removed a brown paper bag. He stared into the bag and sighed,

"Every day, cheese and onion sandwiches...I suppose you will be wanting one."

Jessup shook his head,

"I don't eat much, Sarge."

The Sergeant shook his head,

"So, you don't smoke, and you don't eat." He held the sandwich a bit closer to Jessup, "Are you sure you wouldn't like just to hold it for old times' sake."

Jessup took the offered sandwich and immediately took a huge bite out of it. He sighed contentedly, finished the rest, wiped his hands on his trousers.

"That is the best sandwich I ever ate, Sarge."

"I will tell, Mrs Prichard. I'm sure she will be highly delighted."

He picked up a flask from beside the seat, unscrewed the top and poured himself a cup of tea. Then, seeing the look on Jessup's face, he reached into the glove compartment, removed a battered tin mug, filled that with tea and handed it to Jessup.

"That mug's been around since the Great War," he said. "Took it back to France with me after my first leave. They never used to issue a mug; we had to drink tea from our mess tin. I had burnt lips for the first year of the war. What about you? Did you bring any souvenirs home?"

Jessup sipped his tea and thought about the German Luger and the two rounds of ammunition sitting under his bed, and replied,

"Nothing, Sarge. I don't need reminding of things I'm trying to forget."

To change the subject, the Sergeant said,

"Well, much as I enjoy our little chats, I understand you had something important to show me."

Jessup glanced around the carpark and thought about the story he had decided to tell the Sergeant. He then reached into the inside pocket of his jacket and pulled out the photograph.

Prichard stared at it for some time, as if unable to believe his eyes, then mumbled,

"What have you done, lad? What have you gotten yourself into?"

"It's Grimshaw," Jessup told him. "Every Thursday, he collects money from that man."

He pointed at the other person in the photo and then quickly added,

"It was simply good luck, Sarge. That first time, when you asked me to pay your rent, I popped into a nearby pub. I only had one drink, honestly, Sarge, and I was sitting in a corner, out of the way, when Grimshaw walked in. He didn't see me, but I saw a man give him a bag."

The Sergeant didn't say a word, he just kept staring at the photograph, so Jessup continued,

"Anyway, I got talking to an old chap in there, and he told me that Grimshaw comes in every Thursday to collect the bag, and he said that sometimes he sees him counting money from it."

The Sergeant suddenly turned towards him,

"Who took this photograph?"

Jessup had decided that he did not want to get Bernie any more involved than he already was,

"I did, Sarge, last Thursday. I borrowed a camera off a friend..."

"Are you sure you borrowed it?" Prichard interrupted. "I seem to recall a report coming across my desk about a couple of cameras going missing from a shop down High Holborn street recently. I hope you had nothing to do with that, Jessup."

Jessup tried to look offended.

"Of course not, Sarge. As I say, I have a friend who's interested in photography; I borrowed the camera from him. Then he developed the photo. No one else has seen it."

"And this friend of yours, did he ask what it was about?"

"No, Sarge. He wasn't interested. I took several other photographs of people, and I told him I was just thinking of buying a camera myself."

Prichard rubbed his eyes and then leaned across Jessup and opened the passenger door,

"You know what you have here, Jessup? If this falls into the wrong hands, you have a death sentence. Now listen here, because this is what will happen, you will stay far away from me until you leave and start your new job. Because if I do something about this, and someone says, Jessup was always chatting to the Sarge, then it could end very badly for you."

"Then, let's just throw it away and forget all about it!"

"I wish I could, Jimmy," the Sergeant said, "but you are the kind of man you are, and I'm the kind of man I am, and now I have this photograph, I have to do something about it."

***

Sergeant Prichard made his way through the market until he came to the stall in the corner, selling fruit and vegetables. He dawdled for a moment, checking the quality of the tomatoes, then, when no one was around, glanced up at the chubby man standing behind the stall and said,

"These tomatoes have seen better days, Reggie, a bit like you."

The man smiled nervously,

"Still got a few years left in me yet, Jack."

"I wouldn't be so sure about that, Reggie. You assure me that a bank robbery is going down, I pay you good money, and then nothing happens. How do you think that makes me look? A carload of coppers sitting outside the bank, biting their fingernails, all because I told them that a reliable source had assured me that it would be worth their while."

He stopped speaking as an elderly woman complained to Reggie about the price of potatoes.

"Nothing I can do, love," the stallholder explained, "They have had bad weather there."

"Where?" the lady asked.

Reggie shrugged his shoulders.

"How would I know? Wherever they grow potatoes. I just sell them. I don't grow them."

The lady handed him one potato and a coin.

"Well, I suppose that will have to do then."

As she walked off, Reggie shouted,

"Don't eat it all at once!" Then turned back to the Sergeant.

"If I ever return to a life of crime, it will be because of people like that. Not that I ever will, Jack," then he leaned closer and said,

"You have my word. One minute that bank job was on, and the next minute it was off. It was as if they knew. Not for me to say, of course, but If I were you, I'd be looking a bit closer to home."

Prichard nodded and handed the man three tomatoes.

"Stick them in a bag, Reggie. They're a bit soft, but I will fry them up for tea."

When the man tried to give them to him, he insisted upon paying and then asked,

"Have you heard about any bent coppers?"

The stallholder burst out laughing,

"Have I heard about any bent coppers? What sort of a question is that? It's like asking me if I heard about Father Christmas! Of course, I have."

"Not bread and butter stuff. I mean a copper who is making big money out of it."

Reggie stared back for some time before replying.

"If you don't mind me saying, Jack, are you not getting a bit old for this game? You should retire and spend some quality time with that wife of yours."

The Police Sergeant didn't answer, so eventually, Reggie sighed, and after making certain no one was about, whispered,

"I have heard about someone, now you mention it... Someone at your nick, actually. A Detective Sergeant was what I heard. And that's *all* I heard, and that's *all* I'm saying.'

He turned away and stepped back behind the stall.

"Enjoy your fried tomatoes, Jack."

***

Jessup left the carpark without a backwards glance, made his way home, and quietly opened the door. He thought he could hear snoring coming from Marlow's room, so he sat on his bed thinking about what the Sergeant had said in the car. "You are the kind of man you are, and I'm the kind of man I am."

But what kind of a man am I? thought Jessup. Am I a good person? Am I really trying to help the Sarge, or just feel better about myself?

His mind went back to the outbreak of the war, and Marlow saying that he would not be allowed to join up because he was too young.

"Just lie about your age." Jessup had told him.

*****

Eastbourne, 1940-1942

Marlow left Cripplegate a boy and just a few months later, when the fishing boat had carried them back across the English Channel from Dunkirk following The Battle of France, he could have been mistaken for an old man...his boyish looks replaced by hollowed cheeks and dark circles beneath his eyes.

It was the eyes that bothered Jessup the most.

They had been granted a few days leave, and afterwards, he was pleasantly surprised when Harry met him at the railway station to return to camp.

"I must admit, I thought you would go AWOL," he told his friend. But Harry had smiled, a bit like his old self and said,

"It should be over soon. One day I hope to have a son, and I want him to be proud of me, Jimmy. Remember, you told me that on the day the war broke out."

Jessup tried to recall if he had really meant that or had he just wanted his friend to join him on a big adventure.

Much to everyone's delight, following the evacuation from Dunkirk, the regiment had been assigned anti-invasion duties on the south coast, near Eastbourne. Marlow seemed almost back to his old self, the only disappointment being the news that Maud was still not pregnant.

One evening as the lads were relaxing in their quarters, Private Bixby ventured, "My mother swore by a bottle of Stout every night. She reckoned it's good for the blood, and I have two brothers and four sisters, so there could be something in it."

Scouse Jenkins folded the letter he had been reading, tucked it into his shirt pocket and suggested maybe there was nothing wrong with Maud, and perhaps it was Marlow who needed to drink more Stout.

Some of the lads roared with laughter at this idea, so Jessup quickly changed the subject because Harry had already discussed this fear with his friend.

"These things take time," Jessup said as if he knew something about it. Truth be told, he knew as little about the human body's workings as Marlow did and even less about the female body.

***

Jessup's unit was busy building pillboxes around Eastbourne on the south coast for a couple of months. The sunny weather and gorgeous beaches made war appear a distant memory, and even Marlow seemed to have regained the sparkle in his eyes.

Then, on September seventh, war came to Cripplegate, and in that same instant, both Jessup and Marlow lost their mothers.

Early in the afternoon, the air raid sirens had sounded, just as the boys were heading to the canteen for a mug of tea. There had been so many alerts lately, most of them practice drills, that they were tempted to ignore *it. Then from the south came an approaching thunder and the sky grew dark from the hundreds of German bombers and fighters flying overhead.*

Marlow watched them disappear and mumbled,

"They are heading for London."

***

Despite the now daily attacks, they were given a two-day leave pass to attend the funeral of their mothers. Jessup made several attempts at conversation, but Marlow barely spoke throughout the journey.

After his father died, Harry had become incredibly close to his mother. Jessup himself did not know what to feel. Of course, he had loved his mother, but he had spent most of his life staying out of the house to avoid his father.

Now, Jimmy had trouble recalling any happy memories he could cling to. The long hug his mother had given him when he returned home following the evacuation from Dunkirk seemed to be the closest they had ever been.

Before the train reached its destination, they could see signs of the bombings, but nothing could prepare them for the damage done to the East End. They emerged from the darkness of the underground station into bright sunlight, but nothing looked familiar. Buildings all around them were now just piles of rubble, but incredibly, people seemed to be going about their everyday business.

Amongst the remnants of her home, a lady wearing a long apron was hanging her washing over a pile of bricks. Further down the street, a man, sitting in an armchair, read a newspaper, seemingly oblivious to the destruction surrounding him.

Luckily, a month earlier, Maud and her mother had moved out to Romford to live with a family member, so they avoided most of the devastation, but they had arranged to meet up with Harry to support him. Three people from the same block died that night and were given a joint funeral service.

Jessup had left his friend and made his way to his old home and now he stood across the road surveying the damage. Even though the house next door was destroyed, the only damage he could see to his parents' house was to the kitchen facing the road. Part of the roof was gone, and the window had been blown in. Unfortunately, Mrs Jessup had been gazing through it at the time, waiting for the kettle to boil. A piece of glass had been driven into her throat, and she bled to death on the kitchen floor. Mr Jessup had been safe and sound in the Anderson shelter in the back garden. On the phone, he told Jimmy that even though a raid was taking place, his mother had insisted upon popping into the kitchen and making a cuppa.

Jimmy suspected it had been more his father's idea because on the rare occasions he spoke to his wife, it was usually, "How about a cup of tea..." His mother had always appeared happy to be of some use.

When he walked into the sitting room, his father sat in exactly the same spot he'd been in a few months earlier when Jimmy had come home on leave following Dunkirk. In fact, now he thought about it, his father had rarely moved from that spot for most of Jimmy's life.

"Some men are coming to repair the window."

Not, "How are you, son?" or, "I'm heartbroken about your mother."

"I could have a look if you want, Dad."

"No, leave it. They are not charging anything."

At the service, Jessup noticed Harry dabbing tears from his eyes and wondered why he didn't feel the same way. Maybe the grief would come later.

Three coffins stood before them. His mother would have been impressed. She often told him that people from the East End shared everything, and here they were, even sharing death.

After the funeral, a few people returned to Mr Jessup's house, where he barely mentioned Mrs Jessup, but seemed extremely excited about getting his kitchen repaired.

Jessup walked into the back garden to escape the atmosphere and then checked inside the shed. Everything was just as he had left it. His souvenir from France could stay where it was for now.

He left the house without saying goodbye and met up with Marlow at the train station. They sat in silence for some time before Marlow asked,

"How's your father?"

"I have no father," Jessup replied. "He died during the Great War, only his body didn't realise. It came home and sat in the corner of the house ever since. I have no idea how I ever came to be born. I like to think that my mum had an affair with some exciting stranger, and he is my real father."

Marlow nodded and minutes later said,

"Errol Flynn. Remember we saw him in that movie, Captain Blood...'

Jessup looked confused.

"Errol Flynn. He could be the exciting man that your mother had an affair with. Your real name could be Jimmy Flynn."

Jessup laughed loudly and was delighted when his friend began laughing as well.

"Well, I was thinking of someone like the coalman, but if Errol Flynn happened to be in Cripplegate in 1920, then you could be correct."

***

The following year found the unit hard at work during the week, training and building defences, along the beaches and around Eastbourne. The beautiful beaches they had so enjoyed on first arriving were now just a mass of barbed wire and mines. At the weekends, if they could avoid guard duties, they would be hard at play, drinking in the local bars and fighting the hordes of Canadian soldiers based in the town.

The German planes would fly over almost every day, mainly avoiding the barrage balloons and the shells fired from Anti-Aircraft Command. Occasionally, aerial battles could be seen taking place over the Channel, between Spitfires and Messerschmitt's. Huge cheers would erupt if any German planes were seen going down into the murky waters.

Later in the year, the German raids suddenly changed from day time to night time. Sleep became almost impossible, with sirens blaring, guns blazing, and powerful spotlights transforming night into day. But no one complained, knowing that their families and friends in London and other cities were getting so much worse. In time, the raids became less frequent as Germany turned its attention to Russia.

But on the May fourth in 1942, the planes struck Eastbourne...

Jessup, now a Lance Corporal, had been ordered to take a Bedford truck to the Cavendish Hotel to pick up some supplies. With Marlow in the passenger seat, the camouflaged, three-ton truck headed into the town with Jessup at the wheel.

"Will make a nice change; having a drink in the Cavendish," Harry remarked. The unit had previously been banned from the Hotel for fighting RAF troops.

Jimmy smiled, "There might be time for a quick half, but we will need to get the furniture back quickly. That posh booze-up in the Officers Mess is this afternoon, and evidently, if we don't get back sharpish with the tables and chairs, a few of the big wigs will be standing up, and I don't think some of them are up to it."

"A quick half it is, then," Harry agreed sadly. "We wouldn't want the poor officers standing up all evening, would we?"

As Jessup slowed the truck to allow some young girls to cross the street, his friend started singing,

"Wish me luck as you wave me goodbye..."

Jessup immediately joined in, and they sang so loudly that the girls turned their way and began giggling. Suddenly, the girls' expressions changed, and they ran to the other side of the road...

"Didn't think our singing was that bad," Harry muttered just as they heard a roar above them and saw a massive dark shadow pass over the truck. They leaned forward as a Messerschmitt flew over so low that they thought for a second it was going to land in the High Street...

They watched in shock as the German plane banked to the right, and as if in slow motion, St John's church burst into flames.

Jessup floored the vehicle for the Cavendish Hotel, but halfway there realised the plane had banked sharply and was now heading directly for them, barely missing the rooftops, and firing its machine guns as locals fled for cover. Jessup slammed on the brakes and, without a word, jumped from the truck at the same instant as Harry leapt from his door...

Bullets smashed into the truck's engine, and just as they reached opposite sides of the street, there was a loud explosion as the petrol tank ignited.

Marlow raced across the road to join his friend in a shop doorway, his face paler than usual. All around them they could hear explosions and screams as more enemy planes circled overhead. Several bodies were lying in the road, but the soldiers didn't dare venture from cover until the deafening noise stopped just as suddenly as it had started.

Jessup was the first to move, running into the street to see if he could help anyone, but as Marlow raced after him to help, Jessup stood up.

"There's nothing we can do here, Harry. Let's run to the Cavendish. We should be able to phone through to the camp."

As they set off, Marlow noticed that one of the bodies had been nearly sliced in half by the bullets. Shocked locals began emerging from wherever they had taken refuge, and a pall of dark smoke descended over the town centre.

Several prominent buildings had been struck, and when they ran around the corner and glanced towards the seafront, they were shocked to see the eastern wing of the hotel had been severely damaged. The crowd out front parted as a fire truck approached.

A policeman stood near the hotel entrance but seeing the soldiers in uniform, he waved them on through.

Inside the hotel, everywhere was chaos.

Men were frantically digging into piles of rubble, occasionally stopping to listen for signs of life. Two hurried past them carrying a makeshift stretcher bearing a young man in a tattered RAF uniform drenched in blood.

"You help over there," Harry shouted to Jessup. "I'm going to check those rooms." He disappeared through the smoky haze while Jimmy joined the men searching for survivors.

He had barely introduced himself when there was a massive crash from the side of the hotel Harry had run towards. A vast cloud of dust spread rapidly towards them,

"Everyone outside," someone shouted, and the men Jessup had been assisting ran for the exit. Taking a deep breath, he ran towards the cloud of dust.

His eyes stung and he struggled to catch his breath, but he continued feeling his way around, unable to see more than a few inches in front of himself. Every few minutes Jessup called out his friend's name, then stopped to listen for any sound, anything to indicate that Harry was still alive. He coughed violently as the thick dust entered his nostrils and throat.

Stumbling onto a pile of rubble where a wall had collapsed, he cried out as his knees landed on bricks and stone. He hoped Harry was not beneath the rubble.

Inching his way forward, his hand suddenly made contact with someone's leg. Frantically, he felt around in the darkness and recognised the rough material of a uniform and realised that the person's arm was buried beneath the debris... He dug furiously until finally the soldier was free, then lifted him onto his shoulders and turned to the direction where he could now hear voices.

***

Jessup spent several hours at the hospital; medics attended his cuts and bruises as he tried to control his breathing. Harry, whom he had carried to safety, was kept in for a couple of days, with a concussion and broken arm, as well as many cuts and scrapes.

Harry arrived back in camp with his left arm in a sling and, much to everyone's envy, a letter excusing him duties for a week. The lads were even more jealous when later that day, he waved his two-day leave pass.

"Some blokes will do anything," Scouse Jenkins shouted in disgust.

***

Towards the end of August, as the lads stood around cleaning their kit, Marlow suddenly raced into the room waving a sheet of paper. He was so out of breath he could barely speak.

"You look like Harold Chamberlain," Lofty shouted. "If that is a peace agreement, I hope it lasts a bit longer than the last one."

"It's even better than that," Harry replied. "I'm going to be a daddy."

Everyone slapped their friend on the back and congratulated him, knowing how much he had longed for this news. Until Scouse suddenly said,

"Well, I hate to be the bearer of bad tidings, Harry, but you haven't been home in ages..."

Marlow laughed.

"That's what I said, but I was home after the bombing; evidently, that's when it happened. Maud just wanted to wait until it was certain."

Scouse nodded in appreciation.

"Nice work, young Harry. With a broken arm as well. Was there any Stout involved?"

"Absolutely," Harry told them. "We had a bottle each."

***

As the summer of '42 rolled on, despite them showing little interest, Marlow would keep the lads up-to-date on Maud's pregnancy, proudly reading out every letter.

"You're lucky," Scouse told him. "I was home when Rita was pregnant with our first, and I will tell you what, it was sheer hell. I would much prefer to be on the frontline facing the Germans than go through that again."

Sometimes, despite the occasional bombing raids, they would discuss how lucky they were to have a home posting. Joey "Tiny" Lawrence disagreed.

Joey was the baby of the unit, having joined a few weeks earlier. Though only just eighteen, he was already well over six feet tall and had been known as "Lofty" throughout his schooldays. Unfortunately for

Joey, Lofty Jacobs had joined up the day war broke out and he certainly wasn't going to give up his nickname to some new lad.

So, by popular consensus, and much to the annoyance of Joey, he became, "Tiny" even though he was in fact taller than, Lofty.

Upon hearing them discussing how lucky they were, Tiny said,

"I want to get to the frontline as soon as possible."

"You weren't in France," Marlow told him. "If you had been, you would not be so keen to get back."

"I just want to get out there and do my bit." Tiny insisted.

Jessup let out a loud cheer as he finally managed to remove a splinter from his thumb, then looked up and said,

"If I were you, Tiny, I would be careful what I wish for."

***

Towards the end of the year, they knew something was going on. There was suddenly less emphasis on defences and more on military training. Every day the lads would visit the rifle ranges and then spend many hours taking weapons apart and putting them back together.

Jessup, who had been mentioned in dispatches following the Eastbourne bombing, was now a full Corporal, and much as he enjoyed the slight pay rise, he hated the thought that if things turned sour, he might have to make life and death decisions.

Then, just before Christmas, they were informed that they would be leaving for pastures new in early January.

Their luck had finally run out.

*****

CHAPTER 13

Sergeant Prichard glanced at the clock on the wall… thirty minutes until he handed over to the night shift. He suddenly heard laughter then the two detectives walked past. Grimshaw noticed him, stopped, and leaned against the counter.

"We're just off down The George for a quiet pint to celebrate young Thomas' good news, Jack. He came into a bit of money and just put a deposit down on a lovely new house. You should join us, or is it nearly your bedtime?"

The Desk Sergeant could still hear them laughing after they left the station. He sat down, opened his desk drawer, removed the photograph, and stared at it for a good five minutes. Then he walked down the corridor and tried Detective Sergeant Grimshaw's office door. It was locked as he'd expected. So, from his pocket, he removed a bunch of keys and tried several before finding the correct one. Not many people knew that a spare set of keys for every room in the station was kept behind the front desk in case of emergency.

The office was neat and tidy, tidier than he had expected. He was pretty confident that Grimshaw would not leave any incriminating evidence lying around, but still, it was worth a look. He knew he needed something more than the photograph.

Jack opened the office door and listened carefully. The station was deathly quiet with no one in the cells. It sounded as if everyone was helping the Detective Constable celebrate the purchase of his new home. Jack had a shrewd idea of where Thomas' newfound wealth had come from.

He closed the door behind him, walked over to the filing cabinets and found them locked, so he turned his attention to Grimshaw's desk. There were three drawers on the righthand side. He opened the top one and quickly went through the paperwork inside. Nothing appeared out of the ordinary, so he closed it and tried the middle one, finding only pens, pencils, and various copies of rules and regulations. He shut the drawer and listened for a few seconds, then, satisfied that he was still on his own, pulled open the bottom drawer: reams of paper and a novel, Jack turned it over. *A Murder is Announced* by Agatha Christie.

"So that's what detectives use for training nowadays," he murmured, granting himself a chuckle as he closed the drawer. As he moved away, he noticed that it hadn't entirely closed. He tried a couple of times, then realised that something behind it was preventing closure.

Jack quietly removed the desk drawer and stooped down for a closer look. Taped to the back of the desk, behind the drawer's cavity, was a notebook. He took a deep breath and could feel his heart beating like a drum.

He reached in and peeled back the tape until the notebook came free, then stuck it into his pocket and returned the drawer to its rightful place.

He smiled as it closed perfectly this time and said to himself,

"Always keep a tidy desk. That's what I was taught."

Then he left Grimshaw's office, and just as he locked up, heard a voice from the front desk,

"Are you there, Jack? Sorry, I'm late. Traffic is terrible."

*****

HMS Leopoldville, 1943

Early in January, the Fifth Battalion travelled by train to Gourock on the Clyde and boarded the HMS Leopoldville. Early in the morning, they departed amongst a convoy of other ships of various sizes. Evidently, where they were heading was something they did not need to know. Wedged into a small room were Jessup, Harry, Scouse Jenkins, and Lofty Jacobs, who had all served together in France and been evacuated together from Dunkirk; joining them was Tiny Lawrence.

"This is just great," Scouse complained. "They stick us in a room the size of a toilet with the two tallest men in the battalion."

"I wouldn't complain," Jessup replied. "Most of the lads are sleeping in hammocks up top. I had a word with someone to get us this storeroom, so I would make the most of it if I were you because it is just a matter of time before we are noticed."

As the days passed, the convoy HMS Leo had started with gradually dispersed until they were on their own. The fear of U-Boats amongst the crew was evident in how the ship would zig-zag about instead of sailing a straight course and the strict, "no lights" policy at night. Bets were taken amongst the men as to their destination, with suggestions including North America, Iceland, and one lad who bet that the officers in charge had forgotten where they were supposed to be going, and they would just sail around the planet until the war ended.

Eventually, after keeping them literally in the dark for seven days, they were put out of their misery.

They were heading for North Africa.

Tiny was the only person who seemed genuinely excited by what lay ahead.

"Can't wait to get to Africa and show the Jerrys what's what," he commented.

Lofty winked at the others and said,

"It's not the Jerrys I'm worried about, it's the snakes."

Tiny suddenly looked concerned.

"Snakes, what snakes?"

Lofty looked thoughtful.

"Well, there's the Unger Bunger snake. Evidently, that is nearly as long as this ship and wider than I am."

The colour drained from Tiny's face until everyone burst out laughing.

"Don't worry," Jessup told him. "There are no snakes there."

Then just as a look of relief came over Tiny's face, he added,

"The crocodiles ate them all."

CHAPTER 14

Prichard sat at the kitchen table, studying the notebook. Flo had sat next to the fire, knitting a scarf, until suddenly mumbling,

"Well, I'm off to bed."

Now all was quiet, and he tried to make sense of the figures and the letters, and the dates, that nearly filled the notebook. Jack wrote the dates down on a separate sheet of paper, then checked them against a calendar someone had given them for Christmas.

He suddenly realised that every date occurred on a Thursday. Week in and week out, without fail, every Thursday, and next to it an amount of money and some initials. Then on the opposite page, smaller amounts, and more initials.

Jack rubbed his tired eyes, poured himself a glass of water, and sat back down. Taking his wallet from his jacket pocket, he removed the photograph of Grimshaw receiving money from George Daw, and thought back to when Jessup told him the photo had been taken. He checked that date on the calendar and there it was: an amount of money with the initials, MA, next to it. Of course, The Mackworth Arms.

Another hour and he had deciphered most of the remaining initials as various pubs and clubs in the East End.

He couldn't believe how much money was involved. Grimshaw, and whoever else was in on it, were collecting enormous amounts of cash every Thursday. He wondered what was required in return and noticed his hands were trembling.

***

Jessup entered his flat and immediately noticed the mess in the kitchen. Lately, Marlow rarely came out of his room when Jimmy was around and never thought to clean up after himself. He walked into his bedroom and closed the door, sat down, and removed his boots. Tomorrow was his last day at the station, and on Monday, he would begin his new job. Just the thought of it made him smile.

"It's a new beginning," he mumbled to himself. When he came home from work tomorrow, he would do what had put off for too long. He would say to Marlow,

"It is time to go home, Harry. It's time to let Maud know you are still alive. You cannot stay here any longer."

Jessup dreaded his friend's reaction, but the time had come.

He spotted the metal box lying under the bed, retrieved it, opened the lid, and stared at several bottles of painkillers and the Luger with two rounds of ammunition.

Jessup recalled the times he had stared at that weapon and considered blowing his brains out, and yet here he was, about to embark on a new job, a job where he would get some respect and, who knows, maybe one day even a house and a family.

Steady, Jimmy, don't get ahead of yourself. You know something will go wrong. Something always goes wrong.

Even the pain in his leg did not seem quite as bad as usual. So instead of the three or four tablets he'd been taking lately, he just took one. In the morning, he would keep one bottle and destroy the rest. Jessup stared at the Luger and began to remember, so he punched his leg.

"Don't think. Nothing good ever came from thinking."

Someone had told him that once and it was good advice.

Jessup realised that while the pistol was in his possession, the memories would always come flooding back. Not wishing to throw it in a dustbin where a child might find it, he decided that he'd go to work early in the morning, catch the Sarge in the carpark and give him the pistol.

Jack would know what to do with it.

*****

Algiers Coast, 1943

They wondered how anything could be remaining in, Tiny's stomach. He seemed to be sick every few minutes.

"Not long now," Jessup told him. The ship lay off the Algiers coast, with the entire battalion gathered on deck, waiting to be transferred to the landing crafts.

Tiny wiped his mouth on the sleeve of his uniform and complained that he couldn't swim.

"Best not fall out of the boat then," Jessup remarked.

They watched as the overloaded boats made their way across the rough sea towards the town of Bone. Eventually, Jessup and his friends were part of a group of nearly fifty soldiers wedged onto a craft designed for thirty. All the men were weighed down with extra ammunition, rations, and entrenching tools, as well as their regular water bottles and haversacks.

The landing craft began to bounce around as waves crashed over the heads of the soldiers. Soon they and their kits were utterly drenched, and several men could be seen clutching crosses and mumbling silent prayers.

The noise from the crashing waves was deafening, and most of the soldiers shielded their faces, so it was only *at the last moment that someone began shouting and pointing to the west...*

A lone Messerschmitt was heading straight towards them...

Some of the small craft had already reached dry land, but as Jessup turned his attention away from the enemy plane, he was horrified to see they were still about one hundred yards from safety. Marlow grabbed his shoulder and shouted,

"We are sitting ducks, Jimmy!"

But before Jessup could even react, the plane flew in low and began firing its machine guns. Some of the men immediately jumped overboard, but the weight they carried dragged them beneath the waves.

Jessup turned and was relieved to see Marlow still by his side. Behind Harry, he spotted Scouse, his face as white as a sheet and next to him, Lofty, but there was no sign of Tiny...

For some unknown reason, the German plane flew on and did not return as they feared. Ten minutes later, much to everyone's relief, they were close to shore and disembarked even though the water was chest-high.

Jessup and Harry kept turning to see if they could spot Tiny, but a Sergeant screamed at them to move quickly.

Once on dry land, they reacted as they had been trained, racing across the beach with their rifles in readiness as they headed towards higher ground. But there was no enemy fire, and soon they found cover and lay around in small groups, covering all directions and waiting for decisions to be made.

Despite the warmth of a sunny Tunisian day, men shivered, partly from being soaked to the skin, but mainly from fear of the unknown.

Four soldiers had been lost at sea. Amongst them, Tiny Lawrence, whose war had ended before it had begun.

*****

CHAPTER 15

It suddenly occurred to Jack that the lesser amounts of money must be payments to police officers. Some were immediately obvious: TT must be Detective Constable Terry Thomas, Grimshaw's assistant. Jack thought he knew a couple of others, but the one that concerned him most was the largest sum of money with the initials, BW, alongside it.

He flipped through the pages, and BW always collected the most significant payment. Jack stared across the room and went through the roster of everyone at the station once again, not wanting to believe it. But he finally had to admit that the only person he could think it would be was Bob Watkins, night shift Sergeant and a man Jack had known since he was a young cadet.

At 10 p.m., Sergeant Prichard finally picked up the telephone. It was time to tell the Superintendent what he had learned.

*****

North Africa, 1943

Eventually, orders were passed along the line, and the Company Jessup and his friends were attached to, marched several miles to a narrow, wooded valley and erected tents. Over the next couple of weeks, their temporary home survived two bombing raids and a ground attack by enemy forces before they received orders to move on once more. Everyone was pleased to be leaving this highly vulnerable camp behind, but that did not stop Scouse from complaining,

"Does anyone have any actual plans, or do the powers that be intend just to move us around Africa until they think of something?"

"We will be the last to know," Jessup answered. "Anyway, you know what Tennyson said, 'ours is not to reason why, ours is but to do or die.'"

Scouse was quiet for a moment before commenting,

"Well, I don't know who Tennyson is or what battalion he's in, but that sort of talk could get us all killed."

*****

CHAPTER 16

"William?"

"Is that you, Jack? I hope this is important; I was just going to bed."

Sergeant Prichard told him all about the notebook he had found taped to Grimshaw's desk and what it contained. Superintendent Muller was quiet for some time before replying,

"You realise what you are saying, Jack. You are accusing a fellow officer of taking bribes. Are you certain it couldn't mean something else?"

"Well, I don't know what else it could be. It is dates, initials, and amounts of money. Plus, there is one other thing. I have a photograph of Grimshaw being handed a bag in the Mackworth Arms. Would you like to take a guess who is passing it to him?"

There was a moment's silence, so Jack didn't wait for the guess.

"None other than George Daw. Him and Grimshaw, smiling for the camera. And don't ask me who took the photograph because that is something I will never tell anyone."

Jack could hear the Superintendent take a deep breath. No doubt, he knew that when this came out, questions would be asked about his leadership. Eventually, he spoke again.

"What about these initials, Jack. Do you recognize anyone?"

"One or two, but the one that really threw me was BW. It can only be Bob Watkins. I've known him longer than I have known you; I just hope I am wrong."

Superintendent Muller suddenly came to a decision.

"We can't trust anyone at the station, Jack. Meet me early in the car park, and we are going straight to see the Chief Constable. Bring everything you have, and Jack, well done. I should have listened to you earlier."

*****

Sidi Nsir, 1943

They passed other soldiers who were also on the move, and Jessup hoped they would all be together.

"There is safety in numbers," he thought. But they passed the strategically important position of Beja and carried on northeast until they came to a group of stone buildings, and nearby, a railway line, which Sergeant Tomkins told them ran back to Beja.

"I wonder if I can get a train back to the East End," Scouse muttered.

Standing next to the tracks, they could see a battered wooden sign: "Sidi Nsir".

In the morning, Captain Wilberforce gave a delightful speech. He explained the vital role they would be playing in delaying enemy forces from reaching the strategically important Hunts Gap: they would prevent enemy tanks from crashing through Allied defences to attack Beja.

"We brave men, we band of brothers," he said as if he genuinely believed it... "We will not let that happen."

As they walked back to their tents, Scouse said,

"Have you noticed how everything is strategically important except us?"

"Steady on, Private Jenkins!" Jessup shouted. "Remember what, Tennyson said."

Scouse spat on the ground.

"I haven't even met that fella yet, and already I don't like him."

Later, when they were having a mid-morning cuppa, Marlow asked,

"What do you think, Jimmy? Will we get out of this? My son is due any day now."

Jessup smiled.

"Don't worry, Harry, it will all be over soon enough, and then when we get home, we will visit Captain Wilberforce in his castle or wherever he lives, and we will say, we just popped round because you said we were a band of brothers so we thought you might want to buy us a pint, and he will probably call the police and get us kicked out."

Harry laughed, and Jimmy added,

"Anyway, you do realise you might not have a son; you may have a daughter."

Harry stared into space for a while as if he had not even considered this possibility, then replied,

"If I had a daughter, I would love her just the same. But for some reason, in my dreams, I just see a son."

*****

CHAPTER 17

Jessup woke early, feeling even more anxious than usual. His entire body ached as if he might be coming down with the flu. He quickly dressed, swallowed a painkiller, then stuck the metal box beneath his arm. Before leaving the flat, he knocked gently on Marlow's door and said,

"I have to go to work early, Harry. When I get home, we need to talk."

Jessup waited for a reply but eventually turned away. Just as he was closing the door to the flat, he shouted,

"Keep that kitchen tidy!"

***

Prichard placed his sandwiches in his tattered briefcase along with an envelope containing the notebook and the photograph. Flo had bought the briefcase years ago for him when he had been promoted to Sergeant. He hadn't had the heart to tell her that Sergeants didn't generally carry briefcases... Many were the derogatory comments he'd received when he first entered the station carrying one.

He took a deep breath; this was going to change life at the station, with months, if not years, of inquiries and court cases. Jack was due to retire in six months, but he would ask if that could be bought forward. Even though he knew what he was doing was the right thing, and many officers would agree with him, others would never accept a police officer who had done what he intended to do.

Jack wrote a short note to tell Flo he had gone to work early, then he checked his reflection in the mirror to be sure his tie was correct, then he left the house.

***

Jessup meandered down the street, and for some reason, found himself quietly singing,

"Wish me luck as you wave me goodbye," until he spotted a drain at the edge of the road. He glanced up and down the street, then opened the metal box, removed three containers of painkillers, and dropped them down the drain. When he stood back up, he felt dizzy and noticed his hands were shaking. He decided to get some aspirin after work; the last thing he needed now was to get sick.

Just before he was due to turn right off Commercial Road, he spotted someone climbing out of a car parked across the street. Jessup leapt into a doorway as he recognised Grimshaw, quietly closing the driver's door.

Detective Constable Thomas emerged from the passenger side, and Jessup watched as they looked suspiciously up and down the road, then crossed it and headed towards the police station.

He took his time walking after them, concerned they might turn back and want to know what he was carrying in the metal box. Jessup expected to see them enter the station when he reached the corner, but they were nowhere in sight...

He stood there for a moment, wondering why Grimshaw had parked so far away from the station and why was he here so early? The Detective Sergeant rarely started work before eight a.m.

Jessup knew that Sergeant Prichard wasn't due at work for a while yet but wanted to catch him when he arrived in order to hand over the Luger, so he walked as far as the low wall that ran alongside the station and was just about to sit down and rest his aching leg when he noticed Superintendent Muller's car in the otherwise empty car park.

Jessup scratched his head. He had never known the Super to arrive before nine; something big must be going on. Once he'd handed over the pistol to the Sarge, he would keep an extremely low profile, not wanting any dramas on his last day.

He sat down behind the wall and massaged his leg.

***

Jack parked and immediately noticed William's car in its usual spot: the one with SUPER printed on the tarmac. He could not make out if anyone was in the car, but just as he was about to go check, he heard a quick blast from the car horn.

He reached for his briefcase and opened the car door but then hesitated. He had been a cop for many years, and something did not feel quite right.

Jack glanced around the car park, but nothing seemed out of the ordinary. Eventually, he shrugged his shoulders and pushed the door open, but at the last second, he removed the large envelope from the briefcase and shoved it beneath the seat. Then he shut the case and walked towards the Superintendent's car…

The driver's side door swung open, and Detective Sergeant Grimshaw stepped out, levelling a revolver at Jack's chest.

"Just a quiet chat, Sarge. Get in the back seat."

Jack hesitated until the rear door opened, and he could see young Thomas also aiming a revolver at him. He climbed into the back seat, placed the briefcase at his feet, and said,

"What have you done with the Superintendent?"

But Grimshaw just ignored him, started the car, and drove away from the station.

***

Jessup gasped, not believing what he had seen. After hearing the blast of a car horn, he had struggled to his feet and watched Sergeant Prichard walk towards the Superintendent's car then Grimshaw forcing him into the back seat.

He walked as quickly as he could to Prichard's car, lowered the sun visor, and the keys fell into his hand. Jessup started the engine and raced out of the car park.

There was no sign of the Super's car, so he pressed the accelerator and sped down the road, hoping he was heading in the right direction. Glancing frantically from left to right, he suddenly glimpsed the car down a street on his left.

Jessup skidded to a halt, made a U-turn, and raced after the vehicle. Once more he spotted it, and after closing the gap, he slowed down; the last thing he needed was for Grimshaw to notice the Sarge's car in his rear-view mirror. He took a couple of deep breaths and began to shake involuntarily.

He realised this must have something to do with the photograph and immediately wished he had never gotten involved…

They headed down Wapping Lane towards the river. Jessup knew this area well. It had been devastated during the Blitz, and not much had changed since: primarily bombsites and damaged buildings that were somehow still standing.

Grimshaw had slowed as though he was searching for a particular address, so Jessup hung back and kept the vehicle in sight, but his leg throbbed badly now. He punched it twice, but when he glanced back at the road, the Superintendent's car had disappeared.

Just ahead of him, the mighty River Thames, glinted in the early morning sun…He slowed almost to a stop and frantically looked from right to left and saw them: Grimshaw and Thomas leading the Sarge at gunpoint into a severely damaged building to his left. Jessup could make out the words, Wool Shed, on the side of the building and knew that prior to the war, it would have been bustling, filled with workers unloading and storing bales of wool in preparation for transport to nearby ships.

Jessup quickly parked out of sight and tried to control the violent shaking that had suddenly taken over his body. He tried to open the car door, but his hands refused to move from the steering wheel.

Get a grip, Jessup, move now! The enemy won't go away on their own.

He breathed deeply, removed the Luger from the metal box, checked that it still contained the two rounds then managed to open the car door and make his way to the wool shed. Massive wooden doors on the side, damaged during the bombing, hung precariously, leaving a narrow gap between them.

Jessup carefully negotiated a pile of bricks and rubble next to the gates, and as he drew closer, he could hear voices coming from inside. His palms were sweating so badly now that he had trouble gripping the pistol.

Go away; no one would know. Just leave now while you have a chance.

Instead, he risked a quick glance through the gap in the doors, and was horrified to see the Sarge, sitting on the concrete floor with his left arm handcuffed to a metal pipe. Grimshaw stood over him, his back to Jessup. He had his jacket off, and his sleeves rolled up, and he was punching Prichard in the face…

The Sarge cried out in pain as blood dripped from his nose. Jessup was just about to make a move when he heard a voice from a few feet away and realised that D.C. Thomas was standing just inside the entrance.

"I don't think he knows anything, boss. Let's just leave him. He won't tell anyone."

Jessup stepped back quickly as Grimshaw spun around,

"Shut yer mouth! If you'd checked his briefcase, we would have known he didn't have it on him. There's no turning back now, son."

Then he turned his attention back to the Sarge.

"You know this is the end for you, Jack. I'm going to lock you inside a box and drop you in the river, and then you can see how long you can hold your breath. But it's your missus I'm worried about. Flo, isn't it? If you don't tell me where the notebook and photograph are, I will have to visit Flo and ask her, and if she doesn't tell me where they are, I will have to *make* her tell me, Jack, and I would hate that to happen."

"Okay, okay," Sergeant Prichard cried out. He hated to tell Grimshaw, but if the choice was between his wife and the police, there could only be one winner.

"They're in my car, in an envelope. I stuck it under the driver's seat."

Jessup couldn't believe it; he'd been sitting right on top of it. He glanced once more through the gap in the doors, just in time to see the Detective Sergeant kick an old metal drum in frustration, then stand with his head bowed and his hands on his hips.

"Right, this is what we are going to do. Thomas, take the car back to the station. Check under his driver's seat for the envelope and bring it straight back here. If you are telling the truth, Jack, I will make sure that you get a wonderful police funeral. I may even say a few words myself, what a brave officer you were, that sort of thing, and of course, Flo will be happy with her nice police pension."

He turned back towards the Detective Constable again and shouted, "Well, come on, get a move on!"

The young D.C. stepped through the gap and was just negotiating the pile of rubble, when Jessup suddenly stood up and smashed him in the face with a house brick. He stood over the unconscious police officer and took deep breaths as he watched the blood flow from his head wound.

A car pulled onto the side of the road near the site entrance... Jessup walked towards it, seeing a man arguing with a woman.

He tapped gently on the driver's window and the man jumped with shock and angrily wound down the window,

"What the hell?"

Before he could say more, Jessup pointed the Luger at the man's head and said,

"Go to the Wapping Police Station now. Tell them a policeman is about to be murdered. Tell them to bring an ambulance."

The man remained frozen until Jessup hissed,

"Now!"

Jessup watched the car until it disappeared, then turned back to the wool shed, ignoring the voices in his head

This is stupid, Jimmy. Go home. It's nothing to do with you.

The Detective Constable was still unconscious, his face and white shirt soaked in blood, but Jessup was pleased to see the slight rise and fall of his chest. He stepped over Thomas and carefully peered through the gap in the gates.

Sergeant Prichard was still handcuffed to the pipe; the blood from his face had formed a puddle on the floor. Grimshaw was astride an old wooden box just in front of the Sarge, casually reading a newspaper.

"Just tell me one thing," the Sergeant gasped. "Bob Watkins, is he involved?"

Grimshaw looked genuinely shocked.

"Bob Watkins? He's worse than you are. Why would you think that?"

"I saw the initials in the notebook, BW."

The Detective Sergeant roared with laughter,

"You really are a fool, Jack. B stands for Bill. Bill Muller. BW is our little joke. It stands for Bill's Wages."

Prichard thought how stupid he had been. It suddenly occurred to him that he was probably the only person at the station who called the Superintendent, William.

"Does he know about this?"

Grimshaw appeared to be having the time of his life,

"Of course, he knows. Bill rang me late last night and told me all about it. He told me you were supposed to meet him early this morning. His exact words were, 'Hide his body where it will never be found.'"

Prichard slumped down and closed his eyes, unable to take in what he was hearing.

Jessup had heard enough. He wiped the sweat from his hands, raised the Luger in front of him and crept towards the Detective Sergeant. He tried to hold his hands steady but couldn't stop the shaking.

Suddenly the Sarge opened his eyes, glanced over Grimshaw's shoulder, saw Jessup, and gave a slight shake of his head. But just at that moment, Grimshaw looked up from his newspaper and spotted the movement...

He jumped to his feet and wheeled around with the revolver in his right hand. Jessup fired once, but it struck the wall at the far end of the building. Grimshaw nearly dropped his revolver at the shock of seeing who it was, then raised it to the firing position...

"Don't close both eyes, you idiot. Close the left eye and look down the barrel with your right."

Jessup closed his left eye, looked down the barrel with his right, and shot Grimshaw in the chest.

The Detective Sergeant looked surprised for a moment, then slumped to the ground.

Jessup staggered towards Sergeant Prichard, feeling like he might faint at any moment. He threw the empty Luger aside and quickly retrieved Grimshaw's revolver off the floor and dropped it next to the Sarge, who gasped,

"Thank you," and then shook his handcuffed hand. "The keys are in his pocket…"

Then Jessup saw a look of terror in the sergeant's eyes…

He spun around and Grimshaw stabbed him in the chest with the knife he always wore strapped to his leg. Jessup fell backwards alongside Prichard's feet. Grimshaw dropped to his knees and stabbed Jessup again, then raised the knife high in the air once more, and the Sarge shot him between the eyes with the Detective Sergeant's own revolver.

Jack dropped the gun, reached down with his free arm and cradled Jessup's head as he watched the blood seep from his chest wound.

Sirens approached in the distance.

*****

Outskirts, Sidi Nsir, 1943

Schmidt closed his eyes. He wondered if maybe he could drag this task out for a little longer and just lay here dreaming of home and his pretty wife. But then he heard his name shouted, so reluctantly dragged his weary body from underneath the massive machine, struggled to his feet, spat a mixture of sand, oil, and sweat to the ground, and said,

"That heap of shit is going nowhere."

The tank commander stared at him for a while before shouting,

"I think you mean: 'That heap of shit is going nowhere, Unteroffizier Kruger'!" And I would be careful that the Führer does not hear you talking about his beloved Tiger like that! He will force you to carry it back to the Fatherland."

Schmidt did not reply so Kruger continued,

"So, in your expert opinion, are you saying, that this tank is completely inoperable?"

The mechanic insolently shrugged.

"That depends on what you mean by 'inoperable', Unteroffizier. The firing system is fine. It can still fire shells, but I have no way of repairing the steering

mechanism. We could probably drive it around and around in circles if we wanted to."

Kruger kicked the giant tank in frustration, the pride and joy of the German military. It was considered by many the finest ever built, weighing in at over 50 tonnes and yet as fast as any other tank it was likely to encounter. With almost impenetrable armour and a powerful 88mm gun, it could easily destroy an enemy tank well over 2,000 metres away.

But for Kruger, this masterpiece of German engineering suffered more mechanical failures than any tank he'd ever known. Now covered in camouflage nets, it had reached its final resting place.

The tank commander reached for the binoculars around his neck. At this elevation, he had a perfect view of the surrounding countryside: lush woods leading down to the valley. Kruger could make out a dirt track from the south, which he estimated to be just over a kilometre away.

He turned back to his men and spotted Degler, the cook with the dark eye patch concealing his missing right eye.

"Have you prepared some food?"

The cook quickly snapped to attention.

"I have prepared an exceptional stew, Unteroffizier Kruger."

"And should I ask, what is in this exceptional stew?"

The cook smiled.

"I would prefer it if you did not ask me, Unteroffizier Kruger."

The tank commander came to a decision.

"Get fed and watered, lads, because it may be some time before we get another chance. In thirty minutes, we will move back to the camp, but first we will destroy the Tiger, in case the enemy has a more competent mechanic than Schmidt, and they can get it running again."

The soldiers turned to find some shelter from the blazing sun in which to eat their exceptional stew.

Kruger spotted his gunner amongst them and shouted,

"Baumann, with me, now!"

The gunner ran to his side as Kruger pointed to the tank.

"Is it loaded?"

Baumann nodded.

"I supervised it myself, Unteroffizier."

The tank commander pointed to the valley and said,

"You are fat enough, Baumann, you don't need any more food, so you can sit in your normal position. Line the gun up on the centre of that track, prepare to fire, and if anything, or anyone, appears from the south, blow them back to wherever they came from."

As he walked off, Kruger suddenly felt a tinge of guilt for his gunner, so he turned and shouted,

"Don't worry! I will save you some of Degler's exceptional stew. Why should we be the only ones to suffer?"

***

"What the hell is that?"

"It's a Morris water bowser."

"I know that, but where's the water tank?"

Jessup shook his head,

"See, that is the difference between you and me, Scouse. They just give me orders, and I get on with it. I didn't bother asking them where the water tank had gone because I'm not interested. Someone kindly converted this Morris into a four-seater, so you, me, Harry and Lofty can go sightseeing. Oh, and while we are out for a drive, they would like us to keep an eye out for any German patrols."

On hearing his name, Lofty suddenly showed some interest,

"You want me to sit in that? I will stand out a mile. Where's the armour plating?"

Jessup patted him on the head and said,

"Don't worry, Scouse will be driving so fast that nothing can catch us."

Harry appeared from behind the vehicle and said,

"Well, I will be glad to get out for a drive. I'm sick of the sight of this place already."

*****

CHAPTER 18

Jack was kept in overnight with a concussion and several other injuries. He splashed his face in the washbasin and grimaced on accidentally touching his broken nose.

He opened the door to his room and a young policeman was seated outside reading a magazine. The officer leapt to his feet, dropping his reading material, and stammered,

"P.C. W..Willmot, Sergeant. I was told to keep you safe."

Jack nodded,

"Well, I feel safer already, W..Willmot, just knowing that you are there. Now, have you heard any word on the man who came in with me, Jimmy Jessup?"

Willmot shook his head,

"Sorry, Sergeant. No one tells me anything."

Jack nodded once more,

"Welcome to the police force, lad. Now you just stay here and read your magazine, and I'll go and find someone who knows something."

He started walking towards the reception hall but began feeling a bit dizzy and was just leaning against the wall when a nurse appeared from a room and then ran towards him,

"What are you doing up, Mr Prichard? You should be lying down until the doctor makes his rounds."

"Okay, nurse, but I just need to know what's happened to my friend. His name is Jessup. We arrived in the same ambulance." Jack was insistent.

She gently led him back to his room, and once he was back on his bed, said,

"I'm afraid Mr Jessup is in a very bad way. He is still in a coma. That's all I can tell you. Now I understand, you did not want your wife informed…"

Jack sadly shook his head.

"She was going to stay at her sister's in Brighton overnight, so no point in worrying her."

He lay quietly, trying to fall asleep, but barely ten minutes later, the nurse returned.

'I'm afraid you have some visitors who would not take *no* for an answer."

The door flew open and several high-ranking police officers entered the room. Amongst them, the Chief Constable who said,

"Sergeant, good to see you are looking a bit better than the last time we spoke. Now, obviously, inquiries are ongoing, but we found your car parked up near the wool shed. You will be pleased to hear that several arrests have already been made. It would appear we owe you a debt of gratitude."

He vaguely recalled having a conversation with the Chief several hours earlier and telling him that all the evidence he needed could be found under the driver's seat of Jack's car. It was evident to him now that Jessup must have seen him being kidnapped by Grimshaw and followed them.

Jack stared in the Chief's direction for some time before he answered.

"The point is, sir, I don't know who I can trust anymore."

One of the other officers opened his mouth to speak, but the Chief stopped him.

"If you are referring to Superintendent Muller, you do not need to worry about him anymore. Officers went to arrest him this morning. He locked himself in his office and shot himself in the head. At least he left a detailed letter with the names of everyone involved. No honour amongst thieves. Terrible mess."

Jack wasn't sure whether he was talking about the mess made by the gunshot or the mess made to the force's reputation.

Officers began checking their watches and shuffling their feet, so the Chief Constable said,

"We are all very proud of you, Sergeant." As he turned to leave the room, Jack shouted,

"Sir! The man with me, Jimmy Jessup. He saved my life, Sir."

The Chief Constable hesitated, as if deep in thought.

"The toilet cleaner chap... Well...he did a damn fine job as well."

After the officers left, the nurse returned and asked if Jack needed anything. He shook his head, then changed his mind and said,

"A pen and some paper, nurse. I have a resignation letter to write."

*****

12 miles outside Sidi Nsir, 1943

Baumann settled back in his seat, peered through the turret scope, and scanned the horizon until he spotted the track cutting through the valley. He followed it down and then up the other side where it disappeared over yet another ridge. He adjusted the turret. The tank was now fully primed. Baumann relaxed, rubbed his eyes, and yawned.

*****

Sidi Nsir, 1943

Scouse finished checking the oil and shouted,

"All done, boss! Good to go."

Jessup smiled. He couldn't imagine a day when anyone would ever call him Corporal, and that's the way he liked it.

"Get yourselves fed and watered, lads; I have to go for a briefing. Shouldn't be long now."

*****

CHAPTER 19

An hour or so later, Jack woke up feeling much better. He opened a locker, found his clothes neatly folded inside a paper bag, got dressed, picked up the resignation letter he'd written, and closed the door behind him.

Following several unsuccessful attempts to find Jessup's room, Jack came across a police officer who looked familiar. The officer was seated in a corridor and explained that Jessup's room was on the floor below, and that he was guarding Detective Sergeant Thomas. Jack asked if he could speak with him, and the policeman assented.

Thomas had a large bandage around his head and appeared to be in a deep sleep until he suddenly opened his eyes, saw Jack, and immediately began to weep.

"I had no choice, Sarge. I swear I would have gone and got help, but I didn't know who I could trust. I couldn't believe it when I found the Superintendent was involved. I was scared."

Jack stared down at the man and, for a moment, wanted to relieve his anguish, but instead responded,

"You left me there to die. Jessup was scared as well, but he found the courage to come and save me."

The young detective looked confused, and as Jack turned to leave, he cried out,

"Jessup? You mean that man who cleans the toilets?"

Jack shut the door and headed to the next floor, where he found Jessup lying in a darkened room…

His face was so pale that the scars stood out even more than usual. Several tubes were attached to his chest and arm, and as Jack sat down next to the bed, he could barely make out any sign of breathing. The door suddenly opened, and the nurse he had seen earlier, entered, and stared at him with her hands on her hips.

"I know! I'm leaving now," Jack shouted. "I just wanted to check on my friend, is there any news?"

The nurse gently shook her head, walked over to the bed, and looked at Jessup.

"He lost an awful lot of blood. The doctors did what they could, but it's probably out of our hands now," she said, and then added, "You may want to say a prayer."

The Sergeant slowly stood up.

"If I believed that would help, Nurse, I certainly would. Unfortunately, I've been let down before." He was about to leave when she asked if Jessup had any family because no one else had visited.

Jack thought for a moment.

"He wasn't a big talker, our Mr Jessup. I know his mother was killed in the bombings, but he never mentioned a father." Then he suddenly remembered…

"He told me that an old army friend was staying with him. I wonder if anyone has let him know?" He scratched his chin, then added," Leave it with me."

Once outside the hospital, he wondered what had happened to his car. Jack presumed that it would have been taken back to the station, which would be convenient because he was headed that way to hand in his resignation. But there was somewhere else he needed to visit first.

He walked up Mile End Road towards Jessup's flat. Men were hard at work on the old bomb site: bulldozers shovelled piles of rubble and dropped them into the backs of large trucks. Soon, all the rubble would be gone and replaced by shiny new buildings. Before you knew it, London would be back to normal again. No sign that anything had ever happened, except in the memories of the people who lived through it and one day they would be gone and all that would be left then would be their gravestones.

Get a grip, Jack. You are starting to sound like Jessup.

On reaching the block of flats, Jack noticed a man changing a lightbulb in a stairwell and asked him if he knew where Jimmy Jessup lived.

The man didn't seem interested in replying, so Jack showed his police ID card

"Jessup? Is he the weirdo with the bad leg and the scars on his face?"

"That sounds like the man."

The caretaker wiped his nose on his sleeve, then mumbled,

"Room 12," then turned back to his lightbulb.

Sergeant Prichard knocked on the door several times and then shouted,

"Hello, is anyone there?"

A door opened further down the corridor and an elderly lady stuck her head out.

"I think he works at the police station," and then added, "when he's sober."

"Thank you; I was trying to find his friend, Harry Marlow."

"I don't know anything about that. I hear them arguing sometimes, but I stay out of other people's business."

***

The Sergeant walked back to Arbour Street Police Station and found Bob Watkins was on his own behind the desk. He looked genuinely pleased to see his old friend.

"Glad to see you are still in the land of the living, Jack. I was going to visit with some grapes later.'

Jack smiled and said,

"Well, I'm glad you didn't, Bob. I hate grapes."

He placed his resignation letter on the counter and asked him to hand it to whoever was left in charge. Bob nodded and said,

"If that is what I think it is, I won't be far behind you. It's time we got out. We don't fit into today's police force."

Sergeant Prichard asked if he could check on an address, and Bob waved his hand.

"You do what you want. You are still a police Sergeant," adding, "You know you did a good thing. A brave thing. You and the toilet cleaner."

Jack glanced up from the file he was reading and snapped,

"The toilet cleaner's name is Jimmy Jessup, and he is a braver man than any of us."

He found what he was looking for, made a few notes and asked if he could use the phone. After being passed along by several people, he was finally put in touch with the man he was searching for and arranged to meet in an hour.

"I can spare you fifteen minutes," the man said.

He looked up, and Bob threw him a set of car keys.

"They have finished with that death trap of yours. It's in the car park."

Jack said his goodbyes and left the police station without a backwards glance.

*****

Sidi Nsir, 1943

Jessup raced towards the cluster of stone buildings. He had already been late for a briefing once this week and didn't wish to get into further trouble. A voice suddenly called out, and he recognised Barry Morgan, the Company Clerk,

"Jimmy, I have a message for Harry Marlow. Can you give it to him? I'm a bit busy at the moment..."

He handed Jessup a slip of paper, but just as Jimmy was about to question him, a door opened in the adjacent building and Sergeant Forsythe screamed,

"Jessup! In here now!"

In the Morris fifteen minutes later, Jimmy shouted,

"Okay, lads, let's move! And no fooling about today. Keep your eyes peeled! A patrol spotted tank tracks north of here."

They followed the road north for several miles, and Jessup was pleased to see how alert the lads were, constantly scanning the horizon in all directions. Suddenly, he shouted for Scouse to stop.

The vehicle skidded to a halt.

Jessup ordered the lads to remain seated as he raised the binoculars and scanned the track ahead...

"What's wrong, Jimmy?" Harry asked.

After a moment, he said,

"I'm not happy with that incline up ahead,"

"Can't see a thing!" Lofty shouted from the back seat.

"Exactly, I can't see anything either. Wait here, I'm going to check it out."

Marlow jumped from the Morris and said,

"I will come with you, Jimmy."

But Jessup raised a hand.

"Everybody just wait here; I think I can manage this myself."

Harry shrugged his shoulders and mumbled,

"Yes, Corporal, no Corporal, three bags full Corporal."

Jessup held his rifle ready and kept to the side of the track as he jogged towards the incline. Once there, he made quick progress up the hill and then stopped just near the peak.

As the lads watched from their vehicle, Jessup dived to the ground and dragged himself up until he could peer over the top. He followed the track as far as it could be seen with his binoculars and then looked in all directions, but there was no sign of another human being, let alone any German patrols.

He breathed a sigh of relief, turned, and waved to the lads waiting patiently one hundred yards away. The sun was at its peak and sweat dripped into his eyes. He reached into his back pocket, searching for the dirty rag he kept there for just such an occasion. As he began wiping his face, he noticed that a slip of paper had fallen to the ground, and he suddenly recalled the message Barry Morgan had given him for Harry. He put the rag back in his pocket, picked up the paper, opened it, and read the message.

***

Baumann suddenly opened his eyes, yawned again, and wondered if he'd dozed off for long. He peered through the scope, scanned the horizon, then gasped on seeing a military vehicle parked on the track and a British soldier climb out and jump onto the ground... Panic instantly set in as he considered whether other soldiers had already driven past and were already behind them. He knew there was not a moment to waste.

*****

CHAPTER 20

Jack drove to the underground station, took the tube out to Covent Garden because he knew he'd never get a parking spot, and pushed his way through the mid-afternoon crowds until he reached The Salisbury public house. He glanced above the entrance at the bronze nymphs and then higher at the large clock which told him he was a couple of minutes late. He entered the lounge bar and found it packed with people, but Major Dawson was seated in a corner just as he'd said he would be.

"Sorry I am late, Major; it's been a hectic day."

The man appeared less formal than Jack had expected. He extended a hand and said,

"That's fine. I ordered a couple of whiskeys, hope that is okay with you."

The drinks arrived, and the Major drank his in one gulp, placed his glass on the table and said,

"You were fortunate to catch me at the barracks; we fly out in a couple of days. Now I understand you wanted to know about young Jessup."

Jack nodded but then said,

"Well, he's not so young now."

The Major smiled.

"Of course. I usually only see them as young lads, then they return to civilian lives, and to be honest, I rarely give them another thought. But of course, I remember Jessup. You said on the phone that he'd saved your life?"

Jack finished his drink and proceeded to tell Major Dawson everything that had happened and Jessup's role in it.

"He doesn't appear to have any family. I just hoped you might know some of his old army friends who may wish to visit him."

The Major stared at Jack for a moment, as if he were undecided whether to reveal a confidence or not,

"I visited him at the hospital, you know," he thought for a moment. "In early '44, it would have been. It was a dreadful place. They told me he was slowly recovering from his physical injuries, but mentally, not so good, if you know what I mean. I spoke to him for about an hour, just small talk, the weather, that type of thing. No reminiscing, the doctor had warned me. But all he would talk about was how everything was his fault, his friends dying like that. Rubbish, of course, not his fault at all. It's just war. I heard that he was transferred to a mental asylum after that."

The Major seemed to drift off for a moment.

"His friends did not all die," Jack said. "It turned out one of them had been injured and he had been staying at Jessup's flat. Marlow. Harold Marlow."

The blood drained from the Major's face.

"Is this some sort of joke, Sergeant?"

When he saw Jack's look of confusion, the Major continued,

"Whoever has been staying in Jessup's flat, it certainly is not Harry Marlow. Marlow and the others were blown to pieces by a tank shell in North Africa. I should know. I was in charge of picking up those pieces."

*****

Sidi Nsir, 1943

"CONGRATULATIONS...IT'S A BOY" Jessup read the words twice, grinned, then ran down the hill back towards the truck, waving the slip of paper above his head and shouting,

"It's a boy, Harry! You have a son!"

Scouse, Lofty, and Harry were busy arguing over football teams when Lofty glanced up and saw Jessup running towards them,

"Looks like Jimmy is keen to get back to camp. He must really want his lunch."

Harry stepped out of the truck and as his friend got closer, he realised he was shouting something...

Harry strained to hear...

The wind picked up his friend's words and carried them to him, and he smiled because he knew he was a father, and then Harold Marlow disappeared.

***

Jessup's legs collapsed beneath him as though he'd fallen into a hole...

Marlow smiling and then nothing, just a bright red mist approaching. A flash, like staring into the sun, and then darkness. An incredible explosion and then complete silence.

Jessup tried to drag himself forwards but only managed to move a short distance, and then...

Pitch black.

And Jessup knew a thing or two about blackness.

*****

CHAPTER 21

Jack left the Major to his memories, desperate to be on his own. He walked through an unfamiliar area until he found a quiet public house, then bought himself a glass of beer and sat at a table for one, in a dark corner.

He breathed in the thick aromas of stale tobacco and alcohol and thought about his hero son, shot down from the skies above France. Then, he thought of Harold Marlow, full of hope for the future, blown apart in a foreign land, and of the son who would never meet his father. And finally, Jack thought of Jimmy Jessup, lying in a hospital bed in a coma, with his body full of the reminders of war, and his mind filled with nightmares. He gulped down his beer and left quickly with his head bowed so as no one would see his tears.

***

On the tube, Jack asked someone the time, 5:30. He felt exhausted but had one last visit to make. He drove to Limehouse, to the address he'd written down at the station, and knocked on the door of the old, terraced house. After a few moments, the door opened, and a petite young woman with fierce eyes asked him what he wanted.

Jack explained who he was and why he was there. A young boy suddenly appeared, and she told him to wait in the kitchen.

"Maud, is that Harry's son?"

She nodded.

"Look, Sergeant Prichard. I loved Harry more than anything, but a boy needs a father. I got remarried two years ago to Frank. He treats us well. He should be home soon."

"That's good. I just thought it might help Jimmy to hear a familiar voice. The nurse said that even though someone is in a coma, they may recognise familiar voices.

Maud stared at him and said,

"We were so close, the three of us. It was Harry, Maud, and Jimmy against the world. The man from the army came to see me and told me what happened to Harry, and that Jimmy was in the hospital. I tried to visit him, but they wouldn't let me. Twice I tried, and then a nurse told me that he had given instructions not to let me in."

"I think it was guilt," Jack replied. "For some reason, he blamed himself. It wasn't his fault, but the guilt just grew in his head."

The boy shouted from the kitchen, and she said,

"Got to go now. I have to get my husband's tea ready."

Jack wished her well, but just before she shut the door, he said,

"You know what, Maud? One thing I've realised in the last few years is that some of those who came home were just as dead as those who didn't make it."

As he walked towards his car, Maud opened the front door and shouted,

"I will visit tomorrow! Around lunchtime…"

***

Jack stopped at the corner shop near his house for some tobacco and noticed it was nearly 7 p.m. He wondered if Flo had noticed he was late.

"Not seen you in here for a while, Jack, everything okay? You look like someone's been using you as a punching bag."

He stared back at the man behind the counter, trying to recall his name, and then it suddenly came to him.

"You don't know how right you are, Ron. Still, no point in complaining, is there?"

The man nodded as though he understood, furtively looked about the shop, then said,

"Got something you might like, Jack."

***

He opened the door to his house, and Flo was waiting just inside.

"Where have you been? I rang the station! I've been worried sick, Jack. Look at the state of your face!"

Then she hugged him. They walked into the sitting room and were still hugging an hour later when Jack went to make a cup of tea. He was just about to carry it in when he remembered the bag Ron had given him in the corner shop.

Jack opened it and thought how strange it was that you could miss such unimportant things. Then he placed four spoonfuls of sugar in his wife's cup and watched a smile appear on her face for the first time in many years.

*****

EPILOGUE

Jessup slowly opened his eyes and took in the darkened room, the machines on his left, and the tubes attached to his body. Then he heard a slight sound, glanced to his right and was amazed to see Harry, and beyond him, Scouse, and Lofty looking no older than when he'd first met them.

He struggled to speak for a moment, then gasped,

"I'm so sorry, lads. Have you forgiven me?"

Marlow laughed.

"There was never anything to forgive. We have been waiting for you, Jimmy."

"But I thought..."

"You think too much, Jimmy. Nothing good ever came from thinking."

Jessup suddenly felt all of the pain leave his body, and his strength return. It was as if he were once more a young man.

He smiled and then noticed that Scouse and Lofty were beginning to fade away.

"It's time, Jimmy!" Marlow shouted, and then turned and moved after them.

Jessup threw back the covers, climbed down from his hospital bed, and ran to join his friends.

The End

Evil triumphs when good men do nothing.
Edmund Burke

Other Books by Stephen Ainley
Available Worldwide!

The Dennis Bisskit Adventures

Dennis Bisskit and the Basset Hound
from Beacon's Bottom

Dennis Bisskit and The Man From Paris
With the Very Large Head

www.ingramcontent.com/pod-product-compliance
Lightning Source LLC
Chambersburg PA
CBHW060150130626
46556CB00006B/2584